Far beneath the waters off Ocracoke Island, North Carolina, an ancient evil is awakened, and an archeologist's dream suddenly becomes the world's nightmare.

Hunter Singleton, a reporter for a small-town newspaper, and his estranged wife, park ranger Lisa Singleton, must join forces and battle a presence older than mankind. A being known as Diablero has miraculously reanimated the bones of Edward Teach and is moving relentlessly, day and night, through the dark forests and waterways of northeastern North Carolina. The demon leaves a trail of headless corpses as it slowly makes its way through the swamp to a relic dealer in Williamsburg, Virginia, where it can reacquire what was lost so long ago—the skull that will make it human once again.

But it doesn't stop there. Underneath an ancient church on an island in the Bahamas lies a cave with a secret as fascinating as it is terrifying, and it's Blackbeard's ultimate destination. Hunter and Lisa are joined in their fight by others who say they also seek to destroy the demon. But their true intentions may be less than honorable, and Teach is about to open the gates of Hell on an unsuspecting world.

Then, there are the dreams, strange visions of things that have yet to come to pass, and other visions of unspeakable horror. Teach has to be destroyed at all costs, but how can mere humans stop the unstoppable?

One man knows the answer, a shaman who has plenty of secrets of his own. And he must be found before it's too late. Not only for Hunter and Lisa, but for the entire human race.

Dedicated to my awesome family and to the memory of my father, Marcus Tate, who passed away in May 2009. I miss you, Dad.

Diablero

DIABLERO

Toby Tate
10/23/10

a novel

Toby Tate

2010

This is a work of fiction. The events described are imaginary. The characters and settings are fictitious. Any references to real persons or places are included only to lend authenticity to the story.

DIABLERO

FIRST EDITION

All rights reserved.

Copyright © 2010 by Toby Tate

Cover Artwork © 2010 by Toby Tate

This book may not be reproduced in whole or in part, by mimeograph or any other means, without permission of the publisher, except in the case of brief quotations embodied in critical articles or reviews.

ISBN-13: 978-0-9819572-4-1
ISBN-10: 0-9819572-4-2

Nightbird Publishing
P.O. Box 159
Norcross, Georgia 30091

Website: www.nightbirdpubs.com
e-mail: info@nightbirdpubs.com

PRINTED IN THE UNITED STATES OF AMERICA

First Printing: October 2010

10 9 8 7 6 5 4 3 2 1

Part I
The Death Defier

And there was war in Heaven…
And the great Dragon was cast out,
That old serpent, called the Devil, and Satan…
And his angels were cast out with him.

Revelation 12:7-9

That is not dead which can eternal lie
And with strange aeons even death may die

H.P. Lovecraft—The Necronomicon

The man stepped out of the cypress trees and onto the wet sand, glancing inconspicuously around the beach, then back toward the old Ocracoke lighthouse. He stood not far from the small cemetery on the lighthouse property, which he thought was appropriate, considering the spell he was about to invoke. Sanderlings and seagulls squawked overhead. The sky was overcast with clouds that hid the sun just enough to keep it from being overwhelmingly hot. Amazingly, there was little or no breeze.

Not far away on the horizon, he could see the mast of a small ship, which looked like it might be a fishing trawler, but which he knew was actually a research vessel known as the *Lucille*. He smiled.

He set his backpack down on the sand and began pulling out the various items required for the job—a copper bowl, several small plastic bags, a butane lighter, four short candles, a small plastic bottle of water, and four shot glasses.

One by one he picked up the candles and lit them, casting each to the north, south, east, and west, then set them in a circle in the sand. He filled the shot glasses with water from the bottle and placed each one in front of a candle.

He emptied the contents of one plastic bag, which held ground-up human bone, into the copper bowl, then placed the bowl in the midst of the candles. The man lit the bones with the butane lighter and watched as the flame quickly consumed the contents and died in a curling wisp of smoke.

Sticking the lighter in the pocket of his jeans, he picked up another bag, this one holding moist soil, and poured the contents in a circle around the candles. He put the empty bag in the backpack and picked up the next bag, which held table salt, and poured it in another circle around the soil.

He leaned down, stuffed the last empty bag into his backpack and cinched the top with its drawstring. He stood and adjusted his ball cap, steeling another look around the beach. Satisfied there was no one within earshot, he took in a deep breath and slowly exhaled.

Then, he closed his eyes and quietly began to chant.

Dan Brickhouse lived up to his name—big-boned and built like a tanker truck, which always made it difficult to squeeze into a diving suit. With the help of his friend Jonathan, the expedition's leader and captain of the *Lucille*, he managed to "hat up," get his tanks on and get over the side before the sun had risen too far in the sky. With the time it took for ascent and descent at a depth of three hundred feet, they needed all the daylight they could get.

The mixed gas helmet they used for the dive was not cheap, but getting down to the wreck and seeing it firsthand was a priority for both men, especially considering the identity of the wreck.

For the last two months, they had been searching the waters off Ocracoke Island in hopes of finding a ship that had disappeared nearly three hundred years ago—the *Adventure*, last known to be under the command of Blackbeard the Pirate. Scanning the bottom of the inlet had proved to be an arduous task, like looking for a grain of sand in a swimming pool. But Jonathan was nothing if not persistent. Some would say *stubborn*. He had insisted he knew the whereabouts of the wreck, and that he could find it. In truth, the location of the sunken pirate vessel had come to him in a dream, but he kept that bit of information between himself and Dan.

Jonathan Jefferson's contributions to the field of underwater archaeology had been unmatched on the east coast of the U.S. over the years. He had been instrumental in discovering more sunken ships and their treasures in the Graveyard of the Atlantic than anyone alive. No one in the scientific community doubted his abilities, because he had proved himself time and again.

Jonathan knew that it would be one of the finds of the century, as important as the discovery of Blackbeard's flagship—the *Queen Anne's Revenge*—in Beaufort Inlet some years before.

But hours and days turned into weeks and then months as Jonathan and Dan operated the joystick controls on Robby (Remote Operated Biometric Black and Yellow), a remote access vehicle the team had borrowed from the Oceanographic Institute of Technology out of Virginia Beach. The team searched endlessly over sand and coral, trying to spot the telltale signs of a sunken ship—an anchor, a cannon, a ship's bell, a ship's wheel—but all they managed to get were bloodshot eyes from staring at the PC monitor. They were quickly running out of grant money and had, in fact, come very close to calling it quits.

Then one day, Jonathan finally found something incredible. Not just a ship, but likely the one he had been looking for, sunk into what appeared to be a cavern.

Just like in his dream.

Dan had thought Jonathan was crazy at first. But now, not so much.

With Robby's waterproof, high definition cameras and powerful floodlights, they could see into virtually any space the submersible could get close to. There was also the claw, Robby's remote-controlled hydraulic arm, which they had used days ago to retrieve an old bottle from a hidden compartment inside what they believed to be the captain's quarters.

The hiding place had once been well concealed; a

wooden box built into the bulkhead, similar to a recessed wall safe. It looked as if it had been covered by a small wooden door that would have appeared to the casual observer to be just another part of the wall. It had since partially rotted away, however, and revealed its mysterious contents: an old onion-shaped wine bottle, popular in the early 18th century.

Through concentration, skill and a little luck, Jonathan managed to maneuver Robby through the dark, murky water with only the light from the floodlights to see by, then around through the inside of the ship's hull. The water inside the ship was nearly pitch black, the visibility nearly zero.

Hours later, they finally maneuvered the ROV back to the surface and hauled it aboard the ship with a rusted old winch. What they found inside the bottle, which had been sealed with lead, was even more intriguing. An animal skin at least five hundred years old, covered with blood-red writing in a language neither of them had ever seen.

Jonathan had taken photos of the writing and sent it via e-mail to a friend in Raleigh, someone that he hoped could decipher it. As of yet, they still had not heard anything.

The sea at this depth was dark green from the clay in the soil and an abundance of microscopic life that thrived in the cool water. At three hundred feet, the sun was about the strength of twilight, so an underwater light was a necessity. Dan, an oceanographer by trade, was as fascinated with the structure of the ocean floor itself as he was with the wreck, and used his powerful pistol-grip AquaSun eLED to study any flora and fauna that came within range of the light's beam.

As if on cue, a large red grouper swam by, inches from Dan's face plate, apparently as curious about the diver as Dan was of him, then slowly faded in the distance.

Dan saw Robby move silently around the edge of the cave where the vessel sat covered with barnacles and long tendrils of seaweed, but intact with all eight of her cannons and probably many other artifacts yet to be discovered and brought to the surface.

Though Dan wanted to comment to Jonathan on his various observations, he tried to talk as little as possible, since the affects from the helium in his mixed gas suit made him sound like a munchkin from *The Wizard of Oz*. In fact, upon switching from the nitrox gas mixture to trimix on his descent, he began to sing "Follow the yellow brick road" before he was rudely cut off by Jonathan.

Dan adjusted his weight belt and began to shuffle toward the edge of the cave that yawned like a huge mouth on the ocean floor. He looked forward to each dive, because every day led to another discovery—a ship's bell on Tuesday, a piece of silverware and a dinner plate on Wednesday, a cannonball on Thursday—things that had drifted out of the wreck on its way down to the depths or that had simply washed up out of the cave over the long centuries.

As Dan shuffled along the ocean floor, sand and silt billowing up around his feet, something caught his eye. At first he thought it may be a grouper or a horseshoe crab, and moved in with the light to get a better look. Possibly a manta ray, he thought as he admired the grace and beauty of the creatures.

Dan quickly realized it wasn't any marine life he'd seen before. The creature, or whatever it was, seemed to be digging its way out from under the sand, pushing its way up out of the ground like a mole.

When he got close enough to see what it was, he froze, holding the beam steady, mesmerized by the sight. There were two things pushing sand out of the way now, and something else rising up in the midst of them. A cloud of silt spread out around the thing, partially obscuring it from Dan's view.

Suddenly it broke free of the ocean floor and rose up like a nightmarish monolith, the cloud of dirt swirling in the lamplight like smoke from the fires of Hell.

Dan's last thought before utter panic set in was that the thing standing before him should not, *could not,* be alive.

Without thinking, Dan dropped the AquaSun, then reached down and unfastened his weight belt, letting it fall to the sea floor. He began to rise quickly, ignoring his decompression stops on the way to the surface; but his terrified mind raced beyond logic.

Dan didn't bother switching gases on his mixed gas suit, which resulted almost immediately in hypoxia. He muttered incomprehensibly as Jonathan, who had been monitoring Dan's depth gauges from the *Lucille*, screamed things into the radio that Dan could not begin to comprehend. He ascended in seconds from three-hundred feet to two-hundred-and-sixty feet—two hundred . . . one hundred, his blood filling with gas bubbles and entering his brain, which would soon cause a massive gas embolism.

In a matter of minutes, Dan bobbed to the surface and tried in vain to grab the ladder fastened to the side of the *Lucille*, but his hands no longer obeyed his brain. His eyes rolled in his head like two runaway marbles and he began frothing at the mouth.

Jonathan hoisted Dan out of the water and dragged him across the deck, then laid him out on the deck. With much effort, he pried off Dan's helmet.

The ocean air hit Dan and brought him back momentarily to semi-consciousness.

Dan managed to gain control of his eyes, if only for a second. Just long enough to recognize the face of his friend, Jonathan, who was mouthing words that he could no longer understand.

With every last ounce of strength, Dan grabbed Jonathan by his shirt collar and pulled him close. Something important he had to tell him. Jonathan had to know, had to be made to understand.

Dan forced the words from his brain to his mouth, concentrating every bit of effort into making his lips move, praying to God that he was saying what he meant to say, that Jonathan understood his babbling.

Then, Dan released his grip on Jonathan, lay his head down on the hard wooden deck of the ship, and drifted off into the darkness.

River City, North Carolina
Two Weeks Later

Lisa stepped over the cypress knees and edged her way along the muddy bank of Lake Drummond, following the tracks of a bear that she knew was about to have cubs. The bear, which she had affectionately named Suzie, had been pregnant for months and was soon to give birth. She had seen the black bear foraging in the swamp on several occasions, peering under rocks and inside hollow cypress trees for ants and other tasty morsels. Having been pregnant once herself, Lisa knew exactly how the bear felt. It was all she could do to feed herself, let alone the cubs she carried. Ravenous hunger was a constant companion.

Lisa Singleton had spent much of her time in the lake over the last couple of years as a park ranger, learning the flora and fauna and personality of the Dismal Swamp, its subtle beauty and its hidden dangers. The lake and surrounding forest was a protected wildlife sanctuary spread out over 107,000 acres, and many a hiker and camper had become disoriented and lost in the tangled undergrowth and juniper trees. Occasionally, an old moonshiner or a lost child would die from exposure, unable to cope with the harshness of the dark forest. After sundown, the blackness of night can quickly close in, enveloping the uninitiated like a death shroud, cold and unforgiving.

But people ignored the warnings of park rangers, not fully realizing the sheer size of the swamp until they're too far in to find their way out. That's when the helicopters and search parties got called out, wasting manpower looking for someone who shouldn't have been lost in the first place, had they listened.

Lisa walked along the bank, watching the bear tracks weave from one side to the other as the mama bruin hunted for signs of food. She heard the sound of a woodpecker up above her, and gazed up into the canopy of Spanish moss that hung over her head, partially blocking the midday sun, making it appear later in the day. As she searched for the bird, she suddenly found herself walking in the lake and looked down in time to see her boots filling up with water.

"Shit. That figures."

Thunder sounded in the distance, and she looked to the west. A storm was brewing.

Lisa knew she would spend the next hour walking back to her truck with her feet in wet socks sloshing around inside soaked shoes. Gazing over at the shoreline, she saw the bear tracks continued a ways, then veered off into the forest. The bear had obviously found something interesting.

Lisa turned back to shore when she heard something splash in the water. She looked, thinking a long-nose gar or some other fish had become spooked by her presence. She saw something move beneath the water.

Her curiosity piqued, and knowing that the pants of her khaki ranger uniform would be soaked, she stepped further out into the water to get a better view. She stopped where she had seen the movement and gazed down into the water. The depth was about two feet. Something seemed to glow beneath the murky surface, distorted by the rippling waves. She bent down to get a closer look, and then froze.

Eyes.

A pair of eyes, red and angry, stared up at her from the shallow lake bed. Before she could react, a skeletal hand shot up out of the water and grabbed her by the shirt, then pulled her down into the suffocating darkness.

Lisa let out a short yelp, forcing herself through the thick cloud of unconsciousness until she was able to move her body, then quickly sat up in bed and turned on the bedside lamp.

Her breathing was fast and shallow. She hyperventilated, but she didn't care. Her heart pounded in her chest and beads of sweat stood like dew on her forehead. She squinted at the digital clock. Four a.m. She threw back the blanket on her bed and made her way into the bathroom where she filled a Styrofoam cup with water and drank it down as if she had just crawled through miles of burning desert.

She put the cup down and stared at herself in the mirror. Her dark skin looked pale and clammy. Her black, kinky hair was matted with sweat and her eyes were bloodshot. She appeared to have a hangover, though she hadn't been drinking.

She thought back to the nightmare, but it was mostly just snippets and shadows. Except for those eyes, and the hand.

She didn't know what it meant, but whatever it was, it couldn't be good.

Lisa was now wide awake, and she realized trying to go back to sleep would be futile. She let out a heavy sigh.

"This has long day written all over it," she said to her reflection.

Hunter Singleton sat in his cubicle at the *Daily Tribune*, which had lately become his dwelling place. He had spent so much time here, it seemed, that he hardly ever saw his real home anymore. The sounds of phone conversations, keyboards clacking, and people talking all formed one big cacophony, but to Hunter it was like a symphony. He loved the newsroom, the place where it all happened, where it came together and constituted the daily news. He was a part of the scene, a gear in the wheel of progress.

At least that's what he kept telling himself.

He worked at putting the finishing touches on a story he had been working on for the past few days, a piece centered around some bizarre deaths on Ocracoke Island. A diver from an archeological research vessel had resurfaced too quickly from a dive on the ocean floor and died from decompression sickness, or what divers call *the bends*. He had apparently been frightened by something he had seen on the dive, but no one, including his dive partner, could identify it.

And just a few hundred yards from the beach, an old German Shepherd belonging to a local fisherman, Claude Jenkins, had been found strangled by vines, and cocooned twenty feet up the side of a huge pine tree.

Understandably, the population of the little island was shaken. Death from the bends was not exactly an uncommon occurrence in the ocean, but no one could explain how a dog got up in a pine tree, tangled in the creeper vines like a fly in a spider's web. The sheriff had the usual bullshit line: "The matter is still under investigation." Things like this were not good for tourist season, either, and one thing Ocracoke depended on was the tourist trade.

Hunter had been to the quaint island many times, mainly for R and R, taking in the moonlit nights, the peaceful ocean waves lapping the shoreline, the music of Jimmy Buffet emanating from the front porches of the local residents. Hunter usually stayed in a homey bed and breakfast, close to the nearby shops and restaurants where he could enjoy the best handmade crafts and finest seafood around. The people were friendly, the beer was delicious, and the girls were gorgeous. Of course, there was also the beach. But for Hunter the beach was never more than a place to relax and read a book.

As he pondered over rewriting the lead for his article, the phone on his desk rang. He looked down at the number display and saw that it was his editor. He picked it up on the third ring.

"What's up, boss?"

"Hunter, come to my office. I might have a story for you."

Jeffrey Stanton, Editor-in-Chief of the *River City Daily Tribune*, was a no-nonsense guy, not much in the humor department, but efficient and ambitious. If his paper didn't have it first, then it would have the most. He would dig deeper and find out more than anyone else, sometimes to the chagrin of the story's subjects. With his white hair and perfect teeth, Stanton had always reminded Hunter of Ted Knight, the brash TV anchor from the reruns of the Mary Tyler Moore show he often watched on *TV Land*.

"Be right there, chief," Hunter said.

Stanton hated being called "chief." Hunter figured the only reason Stanton let him get away with it was because he knew Singleton was half American Indian. Hunter would probably never tell him the truth; that it was an affectionate name. Stanton was almost like a second father to him, taking Hunter under his wing as a cub reporter and occasionally even having a beer with him.

He walked through the noisy news room and into

Stanton's corner office.

"What's up, Jeff? Got some new leads for me?" Hunter asked impatiently.

"This one may be a little gruesome," mused Stanton, stroking his chin and staring at a single paper on his desk. "Got a report from the sheriff's office that some guy lost his head, literally, out in the swamp. Some boaters found the body, but no head. I'm afraid you'll have to go down to the Dismal Swamp park ranger's station and check it out, see if you can get a statement. I hate to make you do that, but we need to follow up on this piece before the *Virginian Pilot* or the AP get a hold of it."

Hunter went slack-jawed. "Somebody was beheaded in the swamp? Who the hell would behead somebody in the swamp? Did he get run over by a boat, maybe?"

"That's what I need you to find out. And I need you to make a trip to the coroner's office over in Chesapeake, see what you can find out about cause of death, other than the obvious, I mean. I've already okayed it with them."

Hunter felt his stomach do a back flip. Not at seeing a lifeless body, but at seeing *her*. Lisa Singleton, soon to be *ex*-Lisa Singleton: park ranger, law enforcer, heart breaker. It had been six long months since they'd spoken, and even then it was only to begin divorce proceedings. He would have to swallow his personal feelings, he knew.

But he also thought he just might choke on them.

"Thanks a lot, Jeff."

Stanton managed to look both amused and empathetic. "I know," he said. "I'm a grade-A asshole, but I swear I'll make it up to you. Besides, this could be a really big story, maybe the biggest we've had in a while."

Stanton had a pretty good instinct for what would make good copy and what wouldn't, and Hunter had learned to trust that instinct as well as his own. But Hunter didn't need Stanton to tell him there was something to this story.

Hunter left Stanton's office thinking of Lisa, and dreading seeing her again.

Lisa Singleton, like her soon-to-be ex, was a half-breed. Unlike Hunter, however, she was not adopted, but the product of a loving forty-year marriage between an African-American mother and a Chinese father. She was not only highly intelligent, but painfully beautiful, with full, sensuous lips beneath her small Asian nose, black Asian eyes, and brown skin as smooth as silk. Her one complaint, besides being constantly ogled by men and boys, was the kinky black hair inherited from her mother, and which no one seemed to mind but her.

Her in-your-face attitude was another inherited trait from her mother. Lisa was also a fourth-degree black belt in Wing Chun Kung Fu, which her father had taught her growing up. She still managed to practice daily, and when they were married, she had taught Hunter, who eventually managed to earn his own black belt.

The Dismal Swamp was not somewhere the ranger wanted to be on a bright, sunny day like today, and she slogged through the murky water of Kim Saunders Ditch, searching for something she actually hoped not to find.

The previous night's dream slowly crept back into her mind like a deadly Black Widow spider, until two blazing eyes full of fury cut their way into her consciousness, and she thought she could almost see them staring up at her from the bottom of Lake Drummond.

Just then, a hand touched her shoulder, and she wheeled around in a defensive posture, ready to strike.

It was Hunter. He smiled, disarming her as always. But she was determined to remain distant.

"You know," Lisa said, turning away from Hunter and

continuing her search, "you really shouldn't sneak up on people like that. You could get your ass kicked."

"Yeah, well, you'd be the one to do it, that's for sure," Hunter retorted. "Still keeping in shape, I see."

Hunter looked around at the other people involved in the search. Some wore police uniforms, some were park rangers, and others wore plain clothes. All wore hip-hugger rubber boots, including Lisa. Hunter had borrowed a pair from someone taking a break up on the shore, and slowly waded through the mire, following after his wife, feeling like an outsider.

"Exactly what is it you're looking for, anyway?" Hunter asked, turning his mind back to the murder.

"Don't you know?"

"Some head, right?

Lisa never turned to face her shadow. "Funny. I wish you'd ask me whatever it was you came here to ask."

"A statement about the murder would be a good start," Hunter said.

"A statement? Okay, how about, 'Some guy lost his head and now we're searching for it.' I really don't have much else to say at this point."

Hunter wanted to curl up inside a hole and die, but instead he looked at his wife's long, tightly-curled black hair, which he had always loved, and let his eyes wander down her five-foot-three frame, looking at her shapely back, muscles moving like a prowling panther as she made her way through the water. He remembered how things used to be, and thought about the good times, sitting on the rug in front of the fireplace and talking about where life would take them, about their dreams, about the future.

Unfortunately, this *was* their future.

Hunter gathered up his courage. "Look, can we call a truce? I know it's hard for both of us, but I have a job to do, and part of that job is reporting the facts about this murder."

Lisa could hear the pleading tone of Hunter's voice and

for one moment felt a twinge of regret. A tear began to form in her eye, but somehow she managed to dry it before it fell. She stopped, and turned to face her husband.

"Okay, a truce. Ask your questions, and I'll answer them. Then, I go back to my work, and you go back to yours. Fair enough?"

Hunter stared at her a second, surprised by the anger and the pain that he saw deep within her moist, black eyes.

God, he loved her.

"Fair enough," he said.

Just as he prepared to ask a question, an officer who had been searching along the ditch called out from the shore, near where a tent still sat, the fire from hours before now just a pile of ash.

"Hey, over here!" she shouted. "I think I've found something!"

Doing the best they could to run in knee-deep water and muck, Hunter, Lisa, and the rest of the team waded over to the area where the officer stood staring in wide-eyed shock.

As they gathered together, everyone followed the officer's gaze, and instantly wished they hadn't.

About ten yards from shore, in a patch of juniper trees, was something that looked like a large stone. But as they approached, Hunter realized it was a human head. It lay propped up on one side by a fallen branch, the eyes open but with no pupils, looking like two perfectly white marbles. The skin on the face had a sickly waterlogged grayish-purple sheen. The skin around the neck was ragged and torn, but there was no blood. Hunter imagined that if he touched the face, it would feel like wet leather stretched over a bowling ball.

As he raised his camera to get a shot, he zoomed in for a close-up and saw a white maggot wriggle from out of one of the nostrils and fall to the ground.

Hunter felt his stomach lurch.

He whirled around, put his hands on his knees and threw up a perfectly good ham-on-rye in the brown water of the ditch.

Jason Summerfield read the *Daily Tribune* headline: **River City Man Beheaded in Dismal Swamp** along with its accompanying story, and slowly shook his head, laying the newspaper down on his desk.

He wondered if the police had discovered evidence of a motive, or if anyone even had a clue as to who, or what, they were up against.

He looked out the window as a small moth boat floated by on the Pasquotank River, not really seeing it. He imagined himself in the shoes of the killer, making his way through the swamp, moving toward some ultimate, unfathomable goal. He could hear the sounds of tree frogs and owls all around him, felt the mud squish beneath his feet and the briars and yellow flies on his skin. Saw the green snakes and otters swimming through the waterways, smelled the decay of animal and vegetable matter that permeated the air.

When he moved through the swamp, all became silent, as if its eyes were upon him, watching, terrified.

Summerfield had been to the swamp many times, walking the various man-made boardwalks that wound their way through the forest. Every once in a while he would leave the boardwalk and take a trip off the beaten path, just to make things more interesting, watching and listening for signs of bear or deer. Coming upon a bear cub was a bad move in the swamp, because mama bear was usually nearby and they never took kindly to strangers getting too close to their babies.

Summerfield brought his mind back to matters at hand—the business of the Pasquotank County Museum. He was its head curator, and there was a new exhibit soon to come to its halls, artifacts from the wreck of the *Queen Anne's Revenge*, last known flagship of the dreaded pirate Blackbeard.

Summerfield had obsessively followed the daily online log of the archeological team working the site, which had brought up from the depths everything from cannonballs to wine bottles, gold, even cannons. It was amazing to think that beneath the waves off the coast of Ocracoke Island lay the last vestiges of a man who, in two short years, had created a legend that would last over three centuries. Only a powerful and enigmatic man could do such a thing. Summerfield had often wondered if the remains of the pirate himself could still be buried somewhere in the shifting sands, headless and encrusted with barnacles.

He let out a deep sigh, then looked up at the clock on the wall. It was nearly four o'clock, almost quitting time.

Summerfield logged on to his computer, fired up his search engine, and found the bookmark for the *Queen Anne's Revenge* site to see what new relic had been discovered today.

After spending a few hours following his estranged wife through the Dismal Swamp, searching for the gruesome remains of a beheading victim, Hunter was ready to call it a day, especially after the embarrassment of throwing up in front of her and all those cops.

At least they hadn't laughed at him. *To his face.*

And now, the Chesapeake Virginia coroner's office and a look at a dead body was his next order of business. Hunter wondered what his life was coming to, going from one dead body to the next.

As he drove his Accord down Highway 17, he thought about Lisa. She had cited irreconcilable differences, claiming they could not agree on the simplest things, which had become true in the last few months, especially after the loss of the baby.

Lisa had been seven months pregnant when she began hemorrhaging and ended up calling 911 because, as usual, Hunter had been out working on an assignment that night, and she could not get in touch with him. He had hated cell phones at the time, and refused to carry one. He felt they were dehumanizing and annoying, not to mention expensive.

When he got home, a message on his answering machine from the hospital told him to come to the emergency room. He was frantic.

When he arrived, the baby had already been removed by cesarean. Lisa was alive and sedated, but the baby was dead. He had never even gotten to see it, or to say goodbye.

They already knew it was a girl and had picked out a name, Sophia, as well as readying a room with its various assortments of baby items: a crib, changing table, a small dresser. They had even painted the walls pink, Lisa stenciling it with red butterflies and hearts and the word "love" over and over again. It was a work of art, in Hunter's opinion.

Then their world had come crashing in, one little piece at a time.

Instead of talking about it, however, they boxed it up, afraid to touch the subject as if it were a bomb that might detonate and kill them both.

Lisa blamed Hunter for the tragedy, saying had he been around, maybe it wouldn't have happened, had he been near a phone, had he not been working, had he been more supportive, if only, if only, if only . . .

Hunter could not defend himself, so he didn't even try. He just took the blame and tried not to let his emotions run rampant. He tried to be the rock, the steady voice of calm and reason that held them together.

It did anything but.

Lisa held her rage in for months, until one day she exploded and almost destroyed their house, throwing dishes, pots, pans, and anything that happened to be lying around. Hunter actually caught a few of the projectiles, some with his hands, others with his head.

After that, things went downhill: sleeping in separate rooms, not talking, becoming angry over the slightest things.

Then one day, out of the blue, the separation papers came in the mail. Hunter knew it was inevitable, but somehow it still caught him by surprise. When he confronted Lisa, she looked at him, shaking her head condescendingly.

"Wise up, Hunter. It's time to end the charade," she had said.

That was six months ago. After Lisa had moved out and found an apartment, he began to miss her, and he knew she probably missed him. In fact, he knew she did, but Lisa was too proud to admit it. If anything was to be done, Hunter would have to do it; he would have to make the first move. But his pride was even bigger than hers.

As he drove, thoughts of Lisa burned like candles in his mind, but outside it began to get dark. Hunter still had not driven out of the swamp and had to piss something awful. He pulled over at the next available rest area—nothing more than a picnic table and a trash can—and got out of the car. Luckily, the yellow biting flies had not begun to repopulate in the area quite yet, so he was safe for now. He closed the door, looked both ways to make sure no headlights were visible in the distance, walked behind the car, and unzipped his fly.

A lonely owl hooted overhead, the sound echoing through the swamp like a voice in the wilderness. Hunter looked up into the cypress trees, but saw nothing.

Less than a mile away, deep inside the forest, something inhuman moved through the darkness.

Randy Harrell had worked in the Dismal Swamp most of his life. Farming had once been his mainstay, but then he had turned to moonshining. His father had been a logger, before the government declared the Dismal Swamp a protected wildlife sanctuary. Damned government, always sticking its nose in people's private affairs, taking away their livelihood so some otters can have a place to frolic. It was enough to make a man turn to a life of crime.

Harrell stood at the door of his wooden shack, watching as the powerful alcohol dripped into a glass jug from the end of a long, curling copper tube extending from a huge kettle. Yes sir, another couple of gallons and he'd be set to make a run to Greenville. It seemed people couldn't get enough of his potion, especially those crazy redneck, bed-sheet-wearing KKK goons. Some of the biker gang members and a whole lot of fishermen went in for the stuff, too. Nothing like mixing alcohol and heavy machinery, Randy thought.

Personally, Randy didn't touch the stuff. He had sworn off firewater after watching his old man die from liver disease. There were much easier ways to go out, he thought.

Randy lifted up the front of his ball cap, and mopped the sweat off his forehead with the back of his arm.

"It ain't even hot, yet," he said aloud, thinking about the summer to come.

He looked around at the growing darkness, getting a little spooked by the preternatural quiet.

"Yeah," he said, "it sure is damned quiet out here." Normally, the sound of a million frogs and native birds created a nighttime symphony, one to which Randy had grown so accustomed to over the years, he hardly noticed it any more.

Until it wasn't there.

"Sure is weird," Randy said. "Maybe there's some gators in here or somethin'."

Even so, gators wouldn't frighten birds away unless the birds were in the water. Something strange was going on, and Randy began feeling just the least bit uneasy.

"Cops. I bet the damn cops found my still again, the bastards."

Randy had been busted some 10 years before, but the area he now occupied was secluded enough and off the beaten path that nobody should ever be able to find it, unless they had just stumbled on it by accident.

He decided to not take any chances, however, and went inside to grab his rifle. You never knew what you were going to meet out in the swamp. Maybe a bear, maybe a gator or a rabid raccoon.

The fire Harrell had made gave off plenty of light, and he could see a good ways in every direction, except behind the shack. Somehow, though, he felt the intruder, or whoever it was, was coming from the south, and he held his gun ready.

His head suddenly exploded like a baseball popped with a bat as he was hit from behind with terrific force. Stars filled his vision and he fell to the ground, dropping his rifle in the process. Randy felt his head throbbing and tried to move, lying face-down in the oozing mud and cypress roots. He heard the sound of creaking metal and rolled onto his back, slowly opening his eyes, and saw his rifle, bent into a horseshoe, fall to the ground.

Then he saw what had done it.

It looked like it was human, or once might have been, but that was long, long ago. Randy stared, transfixed, wondering in his reeling mind how this thing could possibly be alive.

Randy tried to make a sound, to scream, to cry out, but nothing would come but a strangled sob.

A rusty sword, which had been hidden in a sheath tied around the thing's body, was silently pulled out and raised over Randy's neck. As he eyed the wide, curved blade, Randy realized with his last sane thought that it looked like something he had once seen as a kid at the local museum—an ancient cutlass.

Randy felt what he thought were snakes crawling over his arms and across his legs, but his eyes told him otherwise. They were cypress roots come to life, pulling themselves up out of the mud like giant, writhing worms. He watched in wild-eyed horror as the roots suddenly tightened like ropes on a torture chamber's rack, and held him fast to the cold, slimy ground.

Then the cutlass came down and put a violent end to his life.

A few dozen yards away in the murky water of a Lake Drummond feeder ditch, a terror-stricken man in a boat watched the event through a thicket of cypress trees, and prayed to God that he hadn't been seen.

Hunter got back into his car after relieving himself beside the Dismal Swamp Canal and picked the cell phone up off the passenger seat. He scrolled through the numbers, found the one he wanted and dialed it.

"Coroner's office," came a female voice, likely a young one from the sound of it. Hunter wondered if she was cute, but a vision of Lisa quickly banished the thought.

"Hi, this is Hunter Singleton of the *River City Daily Tribune*. I just wanted to let Dr. Hodges know I was running late, but I'm on the road right now and should be there in fifteen minutes or so."

"I'll let him know, Mr. Singleton."

Mr. Singleton. God, that made him feel old.

"Thanks," he said and clicked the phone shut.

Hunter Singleton was a young man, but not ignorant to the ways of the world. He had been to battle a few more times than he cared to remember, and had the scars to prove it. Life had never been easy, though he had never complained. Abandoned as a baby, he was left on the steps of the police station at a reservation just outside of Tahlequah, Oklahoma, and taken in by a family in the nearby town. He never found his mother, but eventually figured out from his Caucasian features and dark skin that his father had probably been white, and his mother was likely American Indian.

Hunter loved his family. They had taken him in and raised him as their own, and though they were white, they diligently taught him the ways of the Cherokee. Trips to the library for books about the tribal customs and language, trips to the reservation, videos about what life had been like long before Columbus had set foot on America's shores. Hunter appreciated the history lessons, and the fact that it allowed him to know and understand his roots, to find himself and his identity, and he never forgot it.

There were times as a child when Hunter wondered why his mother had left him. Had he not been loved? Was there something about him that she found so repugnant that she couldn't stand the sight of him? But his father had explained that it wasn't like that. Hunter probably had been loved, otherwise she wouldn't have taken the pains of putting him on a police station's doorstep. It was just the circumstances of life, and her circumstances didn't allow for the raising of a child.

That was something Hunter thought he could live with, so he never asked again. But sometimes, late at night, he would still dream about his mother and wonder how she was and what had become of her.

After high school, Hunter longed to experience life outside the Midwest and the United States. A career in the Navy seemed like the most logical way to achieve that goal, and that brought him east to Virginia. After the Navy, he went to college on the G.I. Bill, and since writing had always been his first love, decided journalism would allow him the chance to write full time.

His first job had been at a weekly newspaper in a small town in North Carolina, doing everything from selling ads to taking photographs and even designing pages. His editor had been a miserable old fart who thought that the world was his enemy, but still Hunter learned a lot, and he loved all of it.

When the reporter's position came open at *The Daily Tribune* the following year, he sent off a résumé and was hired two weeks later. That was three years ago.

Hunter did not relish the thought of seeing a dead body tonight, but the coroner's office had offered, and of course Stanton had jumped at the opportunity to send Hunter to get a look-see. He had seen plenty of dead during his time in the Navy, but never one without a head. He hoped he could hold on to his dinner this time.

He came to the end of the swamp. The highway broke out into open space, surrounded by farmland and covered by a dome of sky the color of blood. From the other direction, cars began turning on their lights, anticipating the coming of night. Better Than Ezra's "One More Murder" blasted out of Hunter's car stereo as he began to think about what he had witnessed on Ocracoke Island. In his mind's eye, Hunter could still see the German Shepherd high up in the pine tree, wrapped in vines as if they were somehow trying to ingest him.

And exactly what had that diver—what was his name, Brickhouse?—seen on that dive that had made him forget everything he had learned as an experienced diver? What made him shoot to the surface like a guided missile? A shark? Unlikely. Whatever it was, getting the bends was less important than getting the hell out of there.

Hunter's gut told him that this death in the swamp and the events on Ocracoke were somehow connected, and it bothered him.

Then, there were the bizarre dreams he had been having, dreams of dark shapes and strange, misshapen beings howling in fury, waiting to break free of a prison that had held them captive for untold eons.

Hunter involuntarily shivered at the thought, then put it out of his mind.

He said a silent prayer as the Chesapeake General Hospital came into view, asking for the strength to see what he knew he didn't want to see.

As Hunter pulled into the parking lot, he saw Lisa's light gray Subaru and winced. His stomach immediately became a knot and he tried to think of a reason for not going inside.

He couldn't think of one.

He pulled up as closely as he could to the M.E.'s section, shut down the car. He sat for a moment, collecting his thoughts, gathering his courage and hoping that everything would go smoothly, and without him saying something stupid, as he often did. If only things hadn't gone this far, he thought. If only we could have been less stubborn, more willing to compromise.

If only . . .

Hunter sighed deeply and opened the door, stepping out into the humid evening air. It was early summer and still getting dark later, which Hunter always liked. It gave him more time to get things done, but of course it also gave Stanton more reasons to make him work late.

Working late—the story of his life.

And to make matters worse, he would now be competing with the *Virginian-Pilot* reporters and radio and television crews. Even *USA Today* would probably take an interest in the story, along with some national TV reporters. At least he still had some inside scoops, like this one.

He checked his back pocket for his reporter's notebook, made sure a pen was in his shirt pocket, and began walking toward the hospital, wishing it was all a dream and he would soon be waking up.

She stood in the hall, just inside the door, waiting for him. Normally, this would have filled him with joy, but under the circumstances, he only felt dread.

"Hey," Lisa said with no sign of emotion.

"Hey," Hunter said back. "Thanks for lining this up for me. Stanton appreciates it, I'm sure. Don't know if I do, though. Never was one for blood and guts."

"Don't worry, there aren't any guts, just blood. Of course, it's all dried up now. And you're welcome."

They walked toward the coroner's office, Hunter noticing the silence and smelling a coppery odor that he felt sure was typical of a medical examiner's office. Whatever it was, it reminded him of death.

They came to a set of double steel doors and swung them open, Lisa in the lead.

"Hey, Doc, our boy finally made it," she said.

After the formalities, the viewing of the actual body was less traumatic than Hunter had expected. Maybe he could chalk that up to his time in the service, or to watching too many horror movies. But somehow, he was able to detach himself from the reality of death and see the body for what it was—an empty shell.

Hunter watched, tense, anxious, as the balding, overworked medical examiner pulled the sheet off the body. Thankfully, Hunter saw that the autopsy had been completed and the chest cavity was sewn back up. The head had been severed, but the wound was ragged, as if cut with a dull cleaver or axe, or maybe a sword. The skin on the edges of the wound had small rips, like the instrument had been not only dull, but covered with some sort of encrustation.

"I ran a test of this green stuff around the wound," the M.E. said matter-of-factly, like a car mechanic explaining a tune-up. "It comes from the sea. Probably barnacles."

"Barnacles?" Hunter asked.

The doctor nodded without looking up, poking and prodding around the headless body like a butcher inspecting a side of beef.

Wherever the weapon had come from, it had been under seawater for a long period of time. Someone had found a sword on a beach, or possibly while diving, and decided to go psycho and decapitate people with it. At least, that was one explanation.

For Hunter, though, it just didn't feel right. There was something about this case he was missing, something important and something bigger than just a freak on the loose. This thing was more than human. It was unnatural, even supernatural.

The M.E. looked across the examination table at Hunter and Lisa.

"Want to see the head?"

The pair looked at each other, then back at the doctor.

"Uh, no thanks. I appreciate your time, though," Hunter said with as much sincerity as he could muster.

The M.E. gave a shrug and pulled the sheet back over the body, hiding it from view.

"No problem. Anytime."

Hunter and Lisa walked back through the steel doors and down the hall to the door leading to the parking lot. There they stood, awkwardly, like two high school kids meeting for the first time.

"Well, thanks for helping me out with this story," Hunter said. "None of the other papers got a scoop like this and I appreciate it."

Lisa smiled and glanced away, unable to look him in the eye.

"Hey, well . . . I'm glad to help out," she said. "I'm not a total bitch, you know. Only when I need to be."

"I never thought you were. Not even once."

She glanced back at him, a slight look of surprise crossing her face, then disappearing.

"Well, I have to get back to work," she said.

"You mean home, don't you?"

"Yeah, I guess I do."

Long silence.

"So, how do you like your apartment?" Hunter finally asked.

She shifted her weight from one foot to the other, crossed her arms and looked down at the floor. "It's okay," was all she could say.

Hunter decided not to prolong their tortured conversation any longer. "Well, I hope you have a good night's sleep and I'll call you later, just see how you're doing.

Okay?"

Lisa glanced back at him, and for a fleeting second Hunter thought he saw joy in her eyes. Or maybe it was his imagination.

"Sure, that would be great."

As he turned to leave, Hunter felt a twinge of hope for the first time in a long while.

Lisa watched as Hunter climbed into his Accord and made his getaway. He never could stand intimate conversation, she thought, and had to smile in spite of herself. Though her estranged husband was in most ways a great lover and provider, when it came to frank discussion or confrontation, he would turn tail and run. Perhaps that was the problem with their marriage.

Was she projecting? Maybe that was her problem, too. Maybe she refused to face the fact that what she saw in Hunter was a reflection of her own shortcomings.

Lisa sighed heavily and replayed their conversation in her mind. She actually hoped he would call her, check up on her. That was what she wanted, though she'd never say it. She wore a tough exterior like a turtle's shell, but inside she was still a woman with emotions and needs that only a man could fill. Her man.

But things got out of hand after the baby died and Hunter just let them happen. He thought Lisa had wanted space, wanted to be left alone, but it was exactly the opposite. She needed him more than ever, and he grew more distant with each passing day. Finally, she had to say "enough." She couldn't let the charade go on any longer, going through the motions like two people acting in a play with no direction. She filed for separation and left home the same day, getting a place in Virginia so as not to accidentally run into him around town in River City.

But it hadn't helped. She felt like hell. To top it off, she felt guilty and she felt sorry for Hunter, leaving him alone when she knew how much he loved her. But she also knew the blame wasn't all hers. Somewhere along the way, Hunter had to take some responsibility.

Maybe he was starting to.

Lisa turned from the door and walked back toward the coroner's office to let the doctor know she was leaving. She opened the steel doors and stuck her head in, purposely avoiding close proximity to the corpse she had seen earlier. One viewing was enough.

"Hey, Doc, thanks for everything. I really appreciate your help. Let me know if anything else comes up, will you?"

The doctor looked over the top of his glasses at Lisa, his hands continuing to work on the body laid out before him as if they had been trained to work without supervision.

"Sure, Ms. Singleton, no problem. Bye, now."

She couldn't tell if he was smiling under the surgeon's mask or sticking out his tongue.

She let the doors swing out and walked toward her car in the parking lot.

The moment she got in the car, her cell phone rang. She pulled it out of her front pocket and flipped it open.

"Singleton here."

"Lisa, we just got a call and thought you might want to know about it."

It was the park superintendent, Jasper Frey, who had been a Ranger since before she was born. He was also her friend and mentor, a man without whom she would not be where she was today.

"What's going on, Jasper?"

"It seems there's been another killing."

"What? This soon? Where did it happen?"

"It was in Virginia. Suffolk, to be exact. It's not our jurisdiction, but they want some help from anyone who knows anything about what's going on. Are you up for it?"

Lisa grimaced, then said the only thing she could say.

"Sure, Jasper, I'm up for it. Where do I go and who do I see?"

"Go to the sheriff's office and talk to Sheriff Sutton.

One more thing you should know, though."
"What's that?"
"This time, there was a witness."

Lisa arrived at the Suffolk County Sheriff's office, already wanting to call it a night. She was running on pure adrenaline.

She pulled her car up to the front door and parked. Since she was still in uniform, she had no trouble getting through to the person in charge, Sheriff Jimmy Sutton.

Though Sutton wasn't a big man, his skin was sun-kissed and his brown hair thick and turning gray. His demeanor gave the impression that he was not to be fucked with. Lisa knew Sutton to be about as old as Jasper Frey and twice as cranky. But he was also an old friend of the family. Sutton and her father had met when her dad was a detective on a case they worked thirty years ago, and the two have been friends ever since. Their favorite pastime was deep-sea fishing, often bringing Lisa along for the ride.

She shook hands, going through the formalities, then told him everything she knew about the case up to that point.

"Well, whoever this guy is, he doesn't seem to be confining himself to North Carolina," Sutton said with a voice that always reminded Lisa of a big diesel truck engine. "He seems to be moving north. He decapitated an old moonshiner close to the feeder ditch. Didn't take anything, didn't do anything else at the scene as far as we can tell. Just killed the guy and went on his way. Oh, and one other thing. The old guy's rifle was bent into a horseshoe."

Lisa wasn't sure she had heard him right. "A horseshoe?"

Sutton held up both hands and made a horseshoe shape with his fingers. "Pretty as you please."

Lisa wondered how the hell anyone could bend a rifle at

all, let alone into a horseshoe.

Sutton continued. "The problem is gonna be trying to figure out where he—assuming it is a *he*—is gonna go next. Any ideas?"

Lisa held Sutton's gaze, feeling a bit uneasy under his scrutiny. "Well, he just seems to kill at random, no rhyme or reason. Nobody has seen him and lived, at least until now. He's not leaving tracks or any kind of clues, just dead bodies, right? He does seem to be moving north, though."

Sutton shook his head, looked down at the ground for a moment, then back up at Lisa.

"The bent rifle wasn't the only weird thing we found."

Lisa wrinkled her brow. "What do you mean?"

"When we got to the scene, we found the victim strapped to the ground. With cypress tree roots."

"Cypress tree roots?"

"Yeah. It was as if they somehow started moving on their own, stretched up out of the ground and grabbed hold of him. Like they were holding him down."

"You're kidding me."

"Nope. And that's not all. Our witness had a pretty wild description of the perp."

"How wild?"

"It was dark and the guy was hysterical. He swears the perp was so thin he had to have been anorexic, and tall, with tattered bits of cloth hanging down and what looked like a big, curved sword in one hand. The witness was paddling down the feeder ditch when it occurred. Said everything got real quiet, and he heard a crack, like something got hit real hard. Figured it was probably the old man's head. He looked through the trees toward where the noise came from, and he could see the campfire and the perp. Said the guy bent the old man's rifle into a horseshoe with his bare hands," Sutton pointed to where the rifle now lay like a metallic pretzel.

"Then he pulled out that sword. The boater didn't stick around long enough to see much more, just got the hell out of there and called 911."

Lisa stood looking at Sutton, trying to take in all that she had just heard, then let out a deep sigh.

"So, what do we do now?"

Sutton turned and looked at the two deputies standing by the office door.

"Jones and Betts, you guys get down to the scene and see what we can do to help out the cops and rangers. Tell the press that a body was found and the incident is under investigation, and that's all. I'll call the police captain and see if they want to set up any roadblocks or checkpoints, though it doesn't sound like this psycho ever uses any kind of vehicle to get around. He does seem to be heading north, though, like you said."

Summerfield read the front page story of the *Daily Tribune* for the third time. There had been yet another killing two days ago, this one in Virginia. There had even been an eyewitness description of the killer, a man who appeared to be suffering from AIDS or anorexia.

He read the statements made by one of the officers assigned to the case, Lisa Singleton. All she said—which Summerfield knew was all she could say—was the matter was still under investigation. In other words, no one knew what the hell was going on.

Summerfield had to smile. Lisa could be coy and evasive, as he knew well. He and Lisa had once been lovers, before they had graduated from community college in Virginia Beach. Afterwards, he had moved on to college and graduate school in North Carolina and she to her career as a park ranger and wife of Hunter Singleton, star reporter. Eventually, Summerfield got a job at the museum in River City and the trio had become friends.

Summerfield stared at the story for another minute, looking at the words, but not really seeing them.

He lay the paper down and faced his computer. After bringing up Google, he typed in two words: *Death Defier*.

Though it could see, it wasn't sight in the traditional sense, for it had no eyes. It walked in darkness, trudging through muck and slime, sometimes completely underwater, always moving, never resting. The path it followed was by sheer instinct, and it moved quickly, whether on land or completely submerged. There was a sense of purpose, a single-minded fury that drove it ever forward toward the goal, the prize that lay ahead.

It was really nothing more than a collection of bones, held together by an unseen force, invisible sinew and ligaments whose tangible counterparts had long ago decayed under the ocean depths. It was covered in green barnacles and imbedded sand that had penetrated its structure and become one with the bone itself. The thing was as much a part of the sea as the sea was of it.

That it had no head was of little consequence. The bones were simply a vessel, an Earthly transport for something not of the Earth, but of darkness. It had a name, but it was a name that could not be translated in any known language. Some called it *Nightmare Walker*, others *Diablero* or *Obeah*. It was myth come to life, and it had been freed from the trappings that had held its secrets for so long, freed by the man with the dark soul. But that didn't matter. What mattered was the prize, and now it was close, very close, so close it could feel it. Soon, there would be regeneration, renewal, and ultimate power.

The thing could sense its energy surge each time it took the life of one of the beings it encountered. The life force flowed from them like a tide from the ocean, washing over it in waves, charging it like a battery cell. Their souls were now part of it, experiencing both the thrill and the horror of its unnatural life.

Memories of its past life filled its consciousness and it took this in, thinking in its own way about the future and the things that would come to pass. It felt emotion; anger, sadness and most of all, hate. It knew that it hated the things called "humans," and therefore had no remorse in killing them. They were simply cattle. The bones that it now occupied were of a man that had once been greatly feared and had made a show of being fearless. But when "it" had come, the man had shown fear. In time, however, acceptance had come, and with it, power and riches.

Then, "they" came, with swords, guns, and determination—determination to destroy it, to kill that which could not be killed. Yet, somehow, it was killed, at least temporarily. For three hundred years, it waited at the bottom of the sea, imprisoned in a mass of waterlogged and decomposing flesh. The fish ate of it, the saltwater corroded its bones, but it survived. It knew that one day, it would again be free to walk the Earth. And then, it would take back that which was lost and free its brothers from eternal darkness.

Since it had been awakened and returned to the surface, it sensed changes in the world, in the attitudes of mankind and in the advancement of science. There were things called automobiles it had "seen" on its journey, and telephone wires that carried the voices of humans for long distances. The humans had advanced technologically, but spiritually they were retreating, becoming more secular with each passing century. It even sensed the wars being fought in the world on a grand scale, dwarfing anything it had seen in its previous life. Though optimism still persisted, the human spirit was becoming battered and bruised.

And that, it thought, would make them easy prey.

John Aiden, a descendent of the early 18th century Governor Eden of North Carolina, considered himself a Virginian through and through. His branch of the family had moved to the Williamsburg area and changed their name shortly after the illustrious governor had pardoned the pirates that had been ravaging the east coast for most of the 16th and 17th centuries. The governor's cousin and Aiden's forbearer gave Eden a piece of his mind and was told that his opinion would be taken under advisement. The next day, the family was packed up and moved to what is now known as Colonial Williamsburg, and there they have been ever since.

His descendents were merchants, trading in dry goods, fabric, medicine, and anything else that would turn a dollar. In the early 1900s, however, they began trading in stocks and bonds, and soon became one of the wealthiest families in southeastern Virginia. So much so that the Great Depression had been no more than a speed bump on the road to success.

Aiden was pushing sixty. His forehead was too big, his chin too small, and his nose too wide. Standing only five-feet-five inches tall, he wore wire-rim glasses and had no taste in clothes, wearing mismatched pants and shirts that usually garnered a good laugh on the golf course.

Despite his perceived physical flaws, Aiden had been propositioned more than once by women, most of whom were interested only in his vast fortune he inherited upon his father's death from pneumonia nearly a decade ago. Aiden's interests did not lie in acquiring wealth or trophy brides, however. One-night stands and prostitutes were the extent of Aiden's love life. After obtaining his Masters in

Biology from the College of William and Mary, he turned his sights on collecting highly-sought-after artifacts, often selling them to museums throughout the world. Some he kept for his own collection. One artifact in his possession was the envy of many in the business.

An avid follower of the news, Aiden had watched with interest and growing alarm the story of a homicidal maniac on the loose in northeastern North Carolina. The killer had made his way up the coastal waterway through the swamp and was now in Virginia. He had so far eluded police and left a grisly trail of headless bodies behind him. The national press ran the story ad nauseum, and even the BBC had taken an interest.

Aiden had never been superstitious or even religious, but he understood one thing—there were occurrences in this world modern science could not always explain. As a scientist, Aiden had seen things that were absolutely astounding. Dead animal cells spontaneously returning to life, cancer cells disappearing without a trace, and many other miraculous events. He believed the killings were not only related to the object he possessed, but that the object itself was the cause.

As Aiden sat in his library behind his large oak desk, he pondered these things. After a moment he swiveled his chair to face a large display case behind him. Positioned between two huge floor-to-ceiling bookshelves, it held some of the most sought-after artifacts in the world of collectors, things for which some had even paid for with their lives. Many were vessels made of gold or silver or some other precious metal. Others were books, so old that a mere touch would cause them to crumble to dust.

Aiden rose from his chair and slowly walked to the case, keeping his focus on one particular item, fascinated by its innate beauty. He pulled a set of keys out of his suit pocket, then unlocked the case and gently slid open the door. He put the keys back in his pocket and reached out to pick up the object that mesmerized and seduced him. It was heavy, solid in his hand, yet the collector knew to drop it would shatter centuries of untold history and forever bar the entrance to a world beyond. He was afraid. Afraid of what might happen, but insatiable curiosity and a need to know far outweighed any fear of death.

Aiden thought back to the day he had tracked this particular artifact down. He had never felt such exhilaration, such complete and profound fulfillment. This was something that was tied not only to the history of the colonial United States, but to his own family as well. He had followed lead after lead, each one coming to a dead end. Yet he had never relented.

Then, the final call had come. The object had been seen in a small town in North Carolina called Bath. He found the town on a map and wasted no time in driving there, checkbook in hand, money no object. He would pay any amount, though he knew it would probably be relatively cheap since the owner likely would not know its value or its origins.

When he finally arrived at the small tavern, the bowl was sitting high up on a shelf behind the bar, rimmed in gold and fitted with a large handle to help accommodate the drinking of excessive amounts of alcohol. It looked almost exactly as he had imagined it from the way witnesses had described it. Of course, he had to authenticate the find, but in his heart he knew that what he was looking at was as real as its original owner once had been.

That was nearly ten years ago, and still the power of what he held in his hand never failed to leave Aiden with a sense of awe.

The skull of Edward Teach—Blackbeard the Pirate.

Hunter sat at his desk staring at a blank computer monitor, wondering exactly how he was going to stay one step ahead of the *Virginian-Pilot*, *USA Today*, the three major TV networks, CNN, and Fox News when his phone rang.

He nearly jumped out of his skin, then snapped back to reality and picked up the phone.

"Singleton here," he said with a little more irritation in his voice than he would have liked.

"Is this Hunter Singleton, star reporter for the *Daily Tribune*?"

Hunter thought the voice sounded familiar, but wasn't sure. "Summerfield?" he ventured.

"Hey, how'd you guess?"

"I'd know that smart-assed tone anywhere. What's going on? Haven't heard from you in a while. Got a new exhibit opening up?"

"Not exactly. It's . . . well, it's a little unusual."

"A little *unusual*? What, did somebody dig up a UFO?"

"Actually, it may be even more bizarre than that."

Long pause.

"Okay. Maybe you could fill me in. What does it concern?"

"I've been following the stories about the murders and I think I may have a little inside information, I guess you could say."

This was getting more intriguing by the second. Hunter switched the phone to his headset and began typing notes.

"Okay, shoot," he said.

"I'm afraid you're going to think I'm crazy."

"Hey, after some of the things I've seen, *nothing* would

surprise me."

"I think your killer is after something, something that probably belongs to a collector who may live in Virginia."

"Really."

"Yeah. I did some research on a whim concerning something I'd read a few years back. It involves a Sonoran Indian legend and something called a Diablero."

"A what?"

"Diablero. It's basically an evil person—if you want to call it a *person*—who practices black magic and can transform itself at will into pretty much any type of animal. Even another person. In Voodoo terms it's known as *Obeah*."

Hunter stopped typing. "You're kidding," he finally said.

"Tell me, have you seen any bizarre, unexplained things that may have seemed physically impossible?"

Hunter thought about the unfortunate diver and the dog on Ocracoke Island, the severed head in the swamp that still caused him nightmares. "Yeah, you could say that," he told Summerfield.

"Then that gives me even more reason to believe my hypothesis."

"Okay, exactly what might that be?"

"I think maybe you should meet me here at the museum. I have a few things to show you that will help convince you and prove that I'm not crazy. Are you free?"

"Sure. I'm on my way."

Hunter hung up and looked at his notes. Now it was getting into sorcery and black magic. What next, the walking dead?

He grabbed his sunglasses off the desk and headed for the door.

Hunter walked up the steps to the Pasquotank County Museum, a brand new structure that had taken a lot of time, patience, and grant money to construct. He had written many a story about it over the years it was "under construction," and often marveled at the fortitude of people like Summerfield who just didn't know when to give up. It was a good thing they didn't, he thought.

Hunter was somewhat in awe of the rustic green, three-story structure that reminded him of an old plantation house with wings, its glass façade reflecting the morning sun and overlooking the Pasquotank River.

He opened one of the glass doors and stepped into the large front hall, eyeing the shad boat suspended from the ceiling ten feet above his head. On a wall to his left were facts and photos of United States presidents born in North Carolina, and to his right the information desk. He said hello to the young lady sitting there, and she told him Summerfield was expecting him.

Hunter made his way up the winding stairs to the second floor and Summerfield's office. Finding the door open, he strode in and saw Jason Summerfield clicking away with his mouse on his desktop Mac, oblivious to his arrival.

The walls were lined with books on every subject, from piracy to antique furniture, glass collecting, and even scuba diving. On one freshly painted wall were Summerfield's degrees from The University of North Carolina at Chapel Hill and Duke University. A painting of Blackbeard's flagship—the *Queen Anne's Revenge,* cannons firing at a long-forgotten enemy—hung on a facing wall. A small mountain of papers cluttered Summerfield's desk. The papers were anchored with a paperweight that looked uncannily like a miniature, gray skull.

After a few seconds, Summerfield looked up, surprised to see Hunter watching him.

"How long have you been standing there?" he asked.

"Long enough. What's the big news? Is it a mummy or a vampire we're dealing with here?"

"Very funny. Here, pull up a chair."

Though they were both in their early thirties, the two men could not have been more different. Summerfield was tall, with short, blonde hair, and decidedly Scandinavian features, which contrasted with Hunter's shorter frame and darker American Indian heritage. With his knack for speaking perfect English, Summerfield gave the impression of being the quintessential college professor. He was in shape, as well, spending at least an hour a day at the YMCA gym before work, and as progressive in his politics as Hunter was traditional.

Despite these differences, however, and the fact that Summerfield and Lisa Singleton had once had a fling back in their college years, the two somehow got along as well as any two could, managing to become friends over the years. As people went, Hunter thought, there couldn't have been a bigger bore or a nicer guy. Not the worst combination.

Hunter also knew that Summerfield was very, very smart and very good at his job of recreating history. Hopefully, he would be able to shed some light on the craziness of the last few days.

He pushed an intricately-carved, antique wooden chair up next to Summerfield and sat. "Okay, Jason, what are we looking at, here."

An animated skeleton appeared on the black screen, running across an invisible landscape, surrounded by skulls that appeared to be laughing and which were partially obscured by smoke. Above all this were the words *The Death*

Defier.

"Wow, that looks evil," Hunter said.

"You could say that. The Death Defier was, or *is*, a being that is addicted to life. He manages to keep his life by receiving energy from other people, usually shamans, or practitioners of the black arts, who provide him with human sacrifices. How he gets this energy is unclear, but I believe it's probably not a pleasant experience for the unfortunate donors. According to legend, the Death Defier has been around for thousands of years, maybe as long as humankind itself, walking the Earth and biding its time."

Long pause.

"Biding its time for what?" Hunter finally asked.

"Well, that nobody really knows. But I believe the wait may soon be over."

"On the phone you asked if I had ever heard of Diablero. What's that got to do with the Death Defier?"

Summerfield turned back to the monitor and clicked on one of the links. Another screen appeared.

"Well, Diablero, or Obeah, are other names for the Death Defier," he continued, "and the name by which he was known by many of his students at the time of the Spanish Conquistadors."

"Students? What, was he teaching a class at Hogwarts?"

Summerfield ignored the remark. "No, but in return for energy, the Death Defier provided secrets to many of the shamans, giving them even more power to do their evil magic and control their followers, perhaps to gain wealth."

"Okay, I think I'm with you so far. So my next question is, what does all this have to do with our psycho? You think he's the Death Defier?"

"Not exactly. You're really going to think I've lost my mind."

"Hey, Jason, I never thought you were playing with a full deck to begin with."

"Well, I believe that at some point, the Death Defier

had made his way to the American Colonies and had amassed somewhat of a following among those of ill repute, mainly pirates. I think that at some point in the early eighteenth century, one of those students decided that learning the tricks wasn't enough; he wanted to be The Teacher. He wanted to be a Death Defier himself. So somehow, he found a way to not only kill the Death Defier, but steal his power as well."

"So wait a minute. Are you telling me that this guy running around decapitating people is a descendent of one of these shamans or students?"

Summerfield turned to face Hunter. "No. I'm telling you he *is* one of the students."

"Yeah, you're right, I *do* think you're crazy." There was a moment of silence while the gears turned inside Hunter's head. "Okay, let's suppose for argument's sake it was an actual student who has been alive for three centuries. Where has he been all this time and what has he—assuming it is a *he*—been doing with his time?"

"I believe I know who this person was when he was alive. In fact, I have read historical documents that prove it almost conclusively. He's been buried in Ocracoke Bay under tons of sand and silt since 1718."

"The Death Defier was buried under tons of sand and silt? I think you're starting to lose me again."

Hunter got up from his chair and began to pace the room, then turned to look at Summerfield.

"Okay, enlighten me with your wisdom. Who do you believe our illustrious psycho Death Defier to be?"

"It could only be one person, someone who put fear into the hearts of nearly every man, woman, and child in not only the American colonies, but England and the West Indies, as well. Someone who lost his head in a bloody battle aboard an English sloop off the coast of Ocracoke Island almost three hundred years ago."

Hunter's jaw went slack as he and Summerfield stared

at each other. Then Hunter spoke the name almost reverently, quietly as a whisper, as if saying it too loudly might awaken the dead.

"Blackbeard."

Hunter sat in stunned silence, trying to come to terms with what Summerfield told him. Blackbeard the Pirate was alive and well in the 21st century and making his way up the coast of North Carolina for Virginia to do God-knew-what.

"Okay, Jason, you make a good case, though I still find the whole thing unbelievable. I mean, a man from the eighteenth century alive today? It's just . . . well, *impossible*. And why now?"

Summerfield straightened in his chair, placing his hands on his knees and looked at Hunter. "Ah, yes, the hows and the whys. I'm glad you asked, because I come prepared, my friend."

Summerfield rose from his chair and crossed over to one of the bookshelves adorning the large office. Hunter eyed his back, wondering what the man would come up with next.

Summerfield reached out and fingered several newer books, then stopped on a decidedly older volume and gently slid it from its place. He turned and walked back to Hunter, seating himself on the edge of the desk next to him, then opened the book and began thumbing through it, looking for something.

"Here it is," he said after a few seconds. "This book was written by one of the descendents of Blackbeard's original crew aboard the *Queen Anne's Revenge*. He told the story of the voyages Blackbeard took after being pardoned by Governor Eden in 1717."

Summerfield prided himself on his knowledge of the age of piracy, and was considered an expert on the life of Blackbeard. He had managed over the years to acquire written materials, including original documents signed by Governor Eden himself, and rare books, many of which were never known to exist, such as the one he now held.

"What many people don't know and Blackbeard himself never spoke of was the fact that after he was pardoned and had decided to make a life for himself in Bath, he met a man he called 'The Teacher.' Apparently, this man was very, very old and had seen things and been places that staggered the imagination. He told tales of watching the construction of the pyramids and of the Peloponnesian Wars, things that no one in the 18th century could have seen. He spoke in strange riddles and had dreams of things that would come to pass. This man gathered a large following—mostly pirates like Blackbeard and his crewmen—and made them his disciples. They gathered where they could, and learned magic and listened to stories of centuries gone by. According to this book, The Teacher had the power to shape-shift and become anyone or anything he desired. He was also able to control his environment, move things at will, cause inanimate things to come alive . . ."

"Sounds familiar," Hunter said.

"Unfortunately, The Teacher, in order to maintain his existence, needed energy, and this energy could only come from one place—other living beings, mainly humans. They would place the victim, usually a wandering vagrant or a prostitute, even homeless children, upon a stone altar at some undisclosed location deep in the swamp and decapitate them with a cutlass. The Teacher would somehow catch the escaping spirit, so the story goes, and reenergize himself with it."

"Lovely. So what happened to this Teacher?"

"Apparently, Edward Teach, or Blackbeard, figured if he killed The Teacher, he would be able to catch his spirit and become a Death Defier himself. I believe that Teach probably crept up on The Teacher as he was sleeping, which The Teacher rarely did, and cut off his head. The rest, as they say, is history. Blackbeard went back to pirating and became even more fearsome. Then he met Captain Maynard of Her Majesty's Royal Navy."

"That's the guy who killed Blackbeard, right?"

"Maynard was the only person who knew what Blackbeard really was, and how to kill him."

"How exactly did he know that?"

Jason shrugged. "People told stories, and the stories got back around to Maynard. Unlike many people, though, Maynard took them seriously."

**Ocracoke Inlet, North Carolina
November 22, 1718**

It was a good day for killing a demon.

The orange ball of sun crept up over the horizon, splashing the high, thin clouds with hues of red and gold. The Atlantic Ocean lay below, spread out like a green blanket, giving no hint of the life that teemed beneath it. Swells of water rose and fell like miniature mountains and valleys, gently rocking the two wooden vessels that dimpled its vast surface. The wind blew cold, sending up a fine salt spray that slowly cocooned everything like a million busy silkworms. Seagulls squawked overhead, indifferent but watchful, floating on gusts of wind as if hanging from invisible threads.

The beaches of what would one day be known as Ocracoke Island did their best to hold back the sea that lapped their shores. Small sanderlings chased tiny crabs to and fro in the wet sand, oblivious to the battle about to take place just offshore.

The irony of a beautiful sunrise on this day was not lost on Captain Robert Maynard. Thinking of what lay ahead, his stomach knotted like a clenched fist. His mouth was dry as dirt. The cold wind bit into his skin like stinging horseflies, only heightening his apprehension. Seamen in stocking caps and breeches groggily made their way to various parts of the flagship to perform their duties, hoping the mundane repetition of their tasks would somehow distract the shadow of death that hovered nearby. But the captain of the Royal Navy, commanding a small armada of only two sloops and a hundred men, dared not show fear, for he knew to do so could jeopardize the confidence of his crew, and that he could not afford.

His eyes watered and burned from the cold as he watched the first mate bark orders to lower a rowboat into the water. The ship swayed in the current, wooden beams creaking as the waves lapped against the side. Though the ship was small, it dwarfed the boat being let down by ropes into the sea. The captain looked to the south over the shoreline of the island, his hands behind him in silent repose. In the distance he could see the main mast of a sloop, the *Adventure*.

Maynard was still a young man, but the years of salt-sea air and relentless sun had aged his skin like tanned leather. He had not been home for some time, and though this particular job would likely prove difficult, he would see it through to the bitter end, and perhaps return home a hero.

Maynard turned as the boat lowered into the water. The wind blew his long ponytail, trying its best to blow his tricornered hat off his head. The sun rose yet another foot over the sea, causing him to squint. The boat splashed down into the frigid water. A few of the crew selected for the journey eyed the first mate.

"Off with you, then," he growled.

The three men obediently turned and crawled through the rigging, unfurling a rope ladder down the side, then climbed in succession over the rail and down into the small dingy. Two men topside passed pistols and a sounding line to the men in the boat, then cast off the lines holding it. They bumped against the side of the sloop, splashing seawater inside as one of the sailors manned the oars and turned toward the shoreline.

Caesar smiled, shaking his head as he listened to the four men joking inside the captain's quarters of the *Adventure*. The loud, slurred speech of drunken conversation was punctuated by raucous bouts of laughter. He continued swabbing the wooden main deck outside, singing to himself an old song his mother taught him when he was a boy.

Where're you bound? Bound for Canaan land,
O, you must not lie, you must not steal, you must not take God's name in vain,
I'm bound for Canaan land.
Your horse is white, your garment is bright,
you look like a man of war,
Raise up your head with courage bold,
for your race is almost run.

Caesar, his mother, father, and nine brothers and sisters had all lived on a large plantation in a one-room, dirt-floored shack in Georgia, working from sun-up until sundown in the tobacco fields of a man named Jefferson. The work was hard, sometimes backbreaking, and the elements were not kind. The sun was like a torch that slowly roasted their skin. Their hands became raw and tobacco-stained from the constant picking of leaves, and their feet ached from walking the endless rows day after day. Those who were too young to work in the fields did other chores around the house and plantation, such as cooking, cleaning, pruning trees, and anything else that needed doing.

Of course, Caesar—whom his mother named after the great Roman emperor, a man revered and feared by many—was the eldest and the smartest. His job was also the hardest, because he was, as his daddy would say in his broken African/English, "the prince and successor to this great kingdom." Meaning that when daddy was gone, Caesar would be the man of the house. Somehow his father had known that life was not only hard, it would likely be short. Stolen from his mother in Africa by his own people and sold to a white man in a strange land, Caesar's father was all the boy desperately did not want to be: enslaved by man and cursed by God.

His mother and father were married by Mr. Jefferson's red-faced Lutheran preacher after his mother was "purchased" by the farmer for a large amount of tobacco. In his own way, Mr. Jefferson was a good man. He was born on American soil to a wealthy land owner, and inherited the plantation. The farmer was not keen on slavery, but found it necessary to run the huge plantation, and to keep the political peace. He even thought about setting Caesar's father free at one time, but instead opted to find him a good wife. Companionship could not be denied a man, no matter the color of his skin or status of life. That was his belief.

When Caesar was sixteen years old, his father died of heart failure, working in the fields on a hot summer day. Mr. Jefferson held a small service for Caesar's father, attended by all ten children and their mother, along with a few other local slaves. He was placed in a casket purchased by the farmer, and prayed over by the Lutheran preacher. The two eldest boys, Caesar and Thomas, dug the grave in the back forty of the plantation and laid their father to rest the very next day. There were no tears.

When he was eighteen, Caesar ran away and headed for what would later become North Carolina. There, he met up with an old pirate named Israel Hands, who had been looking for a crew to man a newly acquired fleet of ships. Hands, a surly man resplendent in breeches, waistcoat, bucket boots, and tri-cornered hat, told Caesar stories of the sea and of vast riches in exotic, faraway lands. Caesar knew almost immediately that he had finally found his calling: piracy. No one cared whether you were white or black, free or slave, male or female, only if you had courage and the ability to handle a pistol and a swab. Later, Caesar would learn the art of the cutlass, how to man a sail, how to chart a course by the stars, how to plunder and how to intimidate. And he would learn from the best: Edward Teach, better known as Blackbeard the Pirate.

Caesar finished swabbing the foc'sle, picked up the swab and laid it over his shoulder, then grabbed the bucket. He stepped down onto the main deck and began to make his way aft when he noticed something on the horizon.

The main masts of two ships were moving in their direction. A rowboat led the way.

Seaman Galloway looked in awe at the pirate sloop as it loomed ever closer, her eight cannons peeking out of its side like huge snakes poised to spit deadly venom. The rowboat seemed like a toy.

Galloway took the cap off his head, scratched his scalp, and slipped the hat back on. "Do you think they see us? They must have spotted us by now."

"Aw, stop your worrying. Even if they see us, they won't fire on a bloody rowboat!" hissed the bosun.

Galloway eyed the bosun incredulously, then looked again at the great sloop, now close enough to see the *Adventure* crudely lettered in white on the side of its wooden hull. He could hear the faintest sound of laughter, as if the men on board were flaunting their contempt for authority, partying and carrying on like Nero while Rome burned to the ground.

Galloway picked up the sounding line and dropped the plumb bob until it hit bottom, marked the line, and brought it back up. He looked at the line thoughtfully, then announced, "Only about three fathoms, but she can make it."

The bosun signaled the great warship following behind, showing the way to traverse safely through the shallow waters.

Suddenly a boom like a thunderclap echoed from the *Adventure*, followed by a splash only yards from the tiny vessel.

They were being fired upon.

"Turn this bloody thing around, and be quick about it!" shouted the bosun. "May the Lord help us!"

The oars hit the water. Both seamen pulled frantically in opposite directions. The boat turned slowly, as if the water had suddenly turned to molasses.

Another boom. *Splash!* A couple of yards closer.

The men glanced nervously behind them, wondering if the next cannonball would hit its mark. The bosun looked ahead at the British Navy vessel as they started moving forward, willing the boat to go faster. The two men pulled on the oars, their muscles burning with the effort.

Boom. Splash! Closer.

Boom. Splash! Closer still.

More frantic rowing as the skiff picked up speed.

Finally, they reached the great warship and were hauled aboard.

The two British ships—the *Ranger* and the *Jane*—drew closer together, preparing for battle. Aboard the *Ranger*, Captain Maynard gritted his teeth, watching as the *Adventure's* first mate ran forward and cut the anchor line with a huge sword.

"Look alive, men! They've cut the line and will try to outrun us!"

The captain, standing on the forward deck, turned and ran aft toward the ship's wheel. "Run up the Union Jack!" he ordered as he took the wheel from the quartermaster. The men below decks rowed as the ship picked up speed. "I need flank speed! Raise the sails!"

The men standing on the yardarms high above decks pulled with all their weight on the ropes, raising the huge sails, which immediately caught the wind and began moving the *Ranger*. The men tied the ropes fast, and scrambled down the ladders to the main deck. They were closing in on their quarry.

Caesar stood with alacrity at his post next to one of the large cannons on deck. Neither he nor anyone else had expected to be challenged in home waters. Two ships, one large and one small, both flying the Union Jack, now chased them. The *Adventure* had raised anchor and was heading north, closer to shore.

Caesar had faith in the captain and knew there was a plan, even if he could not see it. The quartermaster, Thomas Miller, looked toward the shore line, and his expression said he was not as sure as Caesar. Mr. Miller left his post at one of the cannons, and Caesar watched as he ran to the helm and grabbed the captain by the shoulder, pointing to the approaching shoreline. Blackbeard backhanded the quartermaster, knocking him to the deck. Caesar thought to himself, *That's a thing you don't want to do, no sir, you don't want to chide a man such as Edward Teach.*

Their crew was down in number, barely enough to man the sails of this pirate sloop. The two English ships were gaining quickly.

Then, just as Teach had planned, the Navy ships ran into the hidden sandbar, an invisible barrier beneath the murky green water.

"Mr. Miller," the pirate captain hissed as he turned to look down on the sprawled figure of the quartermaster, "I trust in the future you will learn patience for that which you do not understand. Now return to your post."

The quartermaster stood and staggered back to the unmanned cannon, rubbing his jaw and feeling grateful that Teach had not ordered him flogged.

"Ready men!" Caesar heard Teach say. "When I signal, fire into the broadside of them, four of you trained on each vessel."

The men, with gunner Phillip Morton in command, readied themselves, every man lining up his sights on the appropriate ship, turning the powerful cannons, loading the heavy cannonballs and the powder, setting the fuse and lighting the torches.

"On my word, men. Steady, *steady* . . ."

The tension was exhilarating to the captain, and Caesar knew it. Edward Teach was made for battle. He donned his black hat and jet-black hair spilled out over his broad shoulders like a dark waterfall. His beard was braided in five ropes and adorned with red ribbons the color of blood. He was a large man, as tall as Caesar, and wore six pistols in six holsters up and down his massive chest. Blackbeard also carried a great cutlass, a formidable weapon Caesar had seen in action, its long, curved blade gleaming in the sunlight. The figure stood against the blue sky, the wind whipping through his hair, a smile on his face, looking to Caesar like the Angel of Death.

"Fire!"

All eight cannons erupted at once. The deafening boom reverberated off the distant sand dunes. Gulls and egrets took to the skies. The massive recoil pushed the ship closer to the shoreline. The cannonballs broadsided both of the Royal Navy ships, splintering wood and bone alike. Screams of surprise and aguish carried across the water to the *Adventure*.

"Good job, men!" cried the pirate captain. "We'll not turn and run from a fight, though they hound us to Hell!"

Just as Teach spoke, the ship jerked violently and most of the crew found themselves sprawled on the deck. The *Adventure* slowly began listing to port.

Blackbeard turned and looked to the port side as the men on deck ran to the railing and stared down at the sandbar they now found themselves wedged upon.

Miller, standing by the port railing, looked back at the captain, his eyes wide with fear. "Captain!" he said. "We have run aground. We're stuck fast."

Teach turned and squinted toward the pursuing sloop. "Damn!"

He slid his curved cutlass from its metal sheath, the steel blade ringing like a small cymbal. The blade hung loosely by his side as he gazed furtively at each of his crewmen. None of them dared flinch.

"Men, we've come to a crossroad and we're damned if we do or damned if we don't. We'll have to stand fast and fight, or run like cowards to the nearest sand dune. I have never run from a fight, nor will I do so now, but I won't ask any of you to fight that haven't the backbone. It would be better to have one willing man than a hundred cowards on my side."

Deadly silence ensued aboard the ship, the only sounds that of Maynard's beleaguered crew throwing ballast over the side of their own vessel.

Finally, Caesar looked from one side to the other at the men surrounding him. Their faces were worn and haggard, hardened like stone from the cruelty of a life at sea, yet their eyes were full of fire.

Then Caesar turned and faced the captain.

"Just give the word, captain."

Teach grinned from ear to ear, then gave the command to go below and bring up on deck his own special secret weapon—hand grenades. The men began parading up and down the ladder from the hold below, carrying armloads of glass bottles filled with gunpowder, small shot, iron pieces, and lead. Each bottle had a fuse worked into the center that was short enough to give no more than five seconds of burn time. And then, devastation.

Aboard the pursuing sloop, Captain Maynard and the survivors of the cannon attack regrouped and set about carrying their dead and wounded below decks. As they were doing this, Maynard had an idea, a ploy that he had seen used in another battle long ago. He turned to his first mate.

"Mr. Pennington, leave the dead crewmen where they are and order the men to have pistols and swords at the ready, then place two ladders into the hold. Have the crew climb into the hold, save yourself and the bosun. When we are alongside the pirate vessel, I will give the word and the crew will come to the main deck and take their revenge on the pirates. But no one is to touch the captain, Blackbeard. Leave him for me. Is that understood?"

The first mate smiled knowingly. "Aye, sir, it is."

As the ship slowly began moving again, Maynard turned back to watch their forward progress as Pennington barked his orders to the crew. Maynard prayed to God that he and his men would survive just long enough to send Blackbeard and his pirates where they belonged.

To Hell.

Teach and his crew waited, watching anxiously as one of the English ships approached the *Adventure* in the shallow water of the sound. Blackbeard noticed that the crew on board the ship had diminished from its earlier number.

He turned to his first mate. "Get the crew to stand by with the bottles, and throw them on my command at the main deck of that ship."

"Aye, captain. All right, men. On the captain's order, light your fuses and aim at the main deck. And don't drop the bloody things, damn you!"

The ship drew closer, and the sound of the hull cutting through the waves reached the ears of Blackbeard and his men. The captain raised his cutlass above his head, as if readying to cut a mooring line. Breathless seconds passed and he could feel his heart beating against the wall of his chest, like a drummer pounding out a driving rhythm.

The cutlass came down like the blade of a guillotine. The crew of the *Adventure* lit fuses and let loose a barrage of smoking glass bottles. The bombs hit the deck and the sides of the English ship, immediately ejecting their deadly contents of lead and shot in dozens of fiery explosions. The resulting smoke was so thick the damaged ship became nearly invisible, as if it had been enveloped by a fog bank.

Blackbeard eyed the ship as the smoke cleared and saw there were only three living men on the deck. With twenty or so corpses. His bombs had worked. The ship was now so close they could grab hold of it with grappling hooks.

"All right, men. We've knocked them all out, save three or four. Pull it up alongside and board her, then cut them down like the English dogs they are."

At this, Blackbeard's crew cheered boisterously, thinking they had won the battle. They tied off the lines, securing the larger ship to their own, and began climbing over the sides to board, yelling fiercely and firing their pistols.

On board the ship, the stench of death and burnt gunpowder was overpowering. There were holes in every part of the ship, some nearly a foot wide, splintered at the edges like jagged, gaping wounds. The dead lay strewn about in pools of their own blood, some missing limbs or even heads that had rolled into corners of the main deck. The pirates simply stepped over them without a second glance, edging ever closer to the three who remained standing.

As they advanced, the hold of the *Ranger* suddenly burst forth with dozens of men—most with their own swords and pistols at the ready—pouring out onto the deck like water from behind a broken dam.

Teach and his crew of ten were taken aback. This was not in the plan.

The heavily armed English crewmen fell upon the pirates like a pack of wild dogs pouncing on wounded animals. The pirates, though surprised and outnumbered, fought furiously. Swords cut through the air, clanging on impact, steel blade upon steel blade, until the weaker man relented and paid with his life. Tortuous screams of the wounded pierced the island air. Blood spilled like wine from a barrel across the already saturated deck. Combatants slipped on the blood, and fell to the deck, taking a pistol shot to the head or catching the razor-sharp edge of a cutlass on the way down.

Blackbeard himself swung his great cutlass like a windmill, fending off anyone who dared come near, and disemboweling those who did. While swinging his sword with one hand, he pulled single-shot pistols from the bandolier on his chest and discarded them on the deck after firing off a shot.

As the battle waged on, it became obvious the pirates were no match for the English. Many of them relented and jumped overboard, begging for mercy. Those remaining on board fought on, but eventually joined the ranks of the dead now laying two-high in some places.

The pirate captain seemed to be unstoppable, nearly supernatural, withstanding cut after cut and shot after shot. His own blood began to soak through his clothes and run down his legs onto the wooden deck, yet still he refused to quit.

"Damn you! I'll fight you all until the demons of Hell come and drag me away!"

At last, there were none left to fight except for Maynard and Teach, and the two now stood facing each other. Maynard had received only superficial wounds, but Blackbeard had not fared as well. Even so, he was still an imposing figure. His eyes glowed red as burning embers and his mouth curled like a snarling, wild dog.

And Maynard could have sworn he saw fangs.

"So, you've come to kill me," Teach said. His jet black hair and beard were matted with blood and his clothes were torn and ragged, a deep wound corresponding with each rip in the fabric. He swayed slightly as he spoke, but his gaze was steady and his voice tinged with venom.

The crew stood enraptured by this meeting between the two captains, wondering just how it would play out.

Then Maynard spoke.

"I know what you are."

The crew didn't seem to know what to make of this, most believing it to be a reference to Blackbeard's chosen profession.

"Do you?" was all the pirate said.

"I've heard the tales, met the witnesses. I didn't believe it at first, but those I have spoken to are not taken to storytelling and fantasy. Then, there are your followers. Many of them know you as Blackbeard, but perhaps I should call you by your other names. Diablero, Obeah . . . the Death Defier."

Teach stood, cutlass in one hand and pistol in the other. The cold breeze blew across the faces of those on deck, but none of them felt it. They could only watch as the drama unfolded in front of them, not quite knowing what to make of the strange conversation.

"I admire your diligence, captain, and your cleverness," Blackbeard croaked. "And since you know *what* I am, you must also know that I cannot be killed."

Maynard glanced at the bloody, bullet-ridden body of the big pirate and knew that what Blackbeard said was true.

Or at least, partly true.

"I know that what you say is misleading. You *can*, in fact, be killed. If one knows the proper method of doing so."

At this, Blackbeard's eyes flashed with anger and he raised his cutlass to strike Maynard. But before his sword could find its mark, a crewman came from behind and cut Blackbeard across the neck. A spray of crimson bloomed against the cold blue sky. Blackbeard, still holding his cutlass aloft, toppled forward and fell face-first on the deck. One of his pistols fired upon impact and a lead pellet came through the pirate's ribs and struck the starboard side, leaving a small hole.

The men turned and looked at the crewman who had brought down Blackbeard, then began to advance upon the motionless figure sprawled on the deck.

As the crew moved slowly toward the immobile body of Blackbeard, Maynard wiped the blood off his cutlass with a tattered shirt sleeve and slid the sword back into its sheath. He looked down at Teach, and with a booted foot, turned him over on his back. The limp body seemed to weigh a ton. The pirate's face was covered with deep, ugly wounds. The jet-black hair and long, braided beard were matted with blood. His chest was peppered with stab wounds and bullet holes. His face looked as if it was still somewhat young, but a scowl had permanently furrowed the brow. Teach was an intelligent looking man, some might even say *handsome*, even in death.

While the crew stood wondering what to do next, Teach suddenly opened his eyes and looked directly at Maynard. The eyes were deep red, as if filled with blood and fire, yet somehow able to see.

"Ye can't do away with me that easily," Teach said. The voice wasn't human, but sounded to Maynard like the deep-throated growl of a large wolf.

He knew it was the voice of a demon.

Blackbeard lay motionless, as if waiting for Maynard to make his move.

With a great battle cry, Maynard unsheathed his sword and raised it above his head, yet he hesitated.

Blackbeard only continued to stare, grinning as if it was all a grand joke, arms lying limply by his side.

"I'll be back," the pirate hissed, and raised a hand toward one of the pistols on his chest.

Maynard brought the cutlass down in a flash and the razor-sharp blade carved a path through flesh and bone.

"The hell you will!" He stepped aside as the demon pirate's head rolled across the deck, coming to rest against the body of one of Blackbeard's unfortunate crewmen. Maynard grabbed the black hair and hoisted the head like a trophy of wild game. He handed it to his quartermaster and ordered it hung from the bow sprit.

An informal autopsy by the ship's surgeon showed that Teach had withstood some forty sword wounds and had been shot at least a dozen times, many of the wounds being potentially fatal.

As the surgeon sewed the chest cavity back together, he shook his head in disbelief. "It's unnatural," he said.

Maynard slid Blackbeard's cutlass back into its sheath, then ordered four of his men to drag the pirate out and toss his lifeless body over the side.

The men carried the dead weight, dripping thick blood and gore across the wooden deck as they went, then heaved the body up over the railing and watched as gravity pulled it down into the frigid water.

As the crew assembled by the railing, Maynard heard several of them cry out, some invoking the name of Christ, others simply cursing in dismay. Maynard quickly stepped up to the railing and looked down. The sight was one that would awaken him from sleep for many years to come.

Blackbeard's headless body swam along the ship's keel, a damned soul defying death to the last, leaving behind a gruesome slick of blood on the water's surface.

As the horrified crew watched, moving from the port side to the starboard side and back, the living corpse swam hand over hand until it had circled the ship three times, then sank into the cold, indifferent Atlantic.

After Summerfield finished his abbreviated, and somewhat animated, version of the life and death of Blackbeard, Hunter could only sit and shake his head. That a man could lead such a life and die such a gruesome death was unbelievable in itself, yet he knew from history that the story was true. At least, the parts leading up to the pirate captain swimming around the ship without a head. After all he had witnessed, however, even that didn't sound crazy anymore.

Hunter eyed the ancient book lying on Jason's desk. "Can I take a look at that?" he asked, nodding toward the book.

Jason glanced down, then picked up the dusty volume and reluctantly handed it to Hunter. "Be careful. This book is older than the United States, and very fragile."

Hunter flipped gingerly through the pages and saw that it was nicely typeset and written in the poetic English of the age of enlightenment. The paper was as thin as onion skin. The writing reminded him somewhat of Thomas Paine, the 18th century rebel credited with starting the American Revolution.

"Who wrote this, anyway? You said it was one of Blackbeard's crew?"

"Yes. Caesar Jefferson, one of the few members of his crew that wasn't hanged. Caesar actually remained onboard the *Adventure*, and was told to blow it up if the pirates were defeated. Before he could do it, though, he was found and subdued by the British troops. Apparently, he was told about the battle on board Maynard's ship by some of the Brits. When he later learned to read and write, he made quite a name for himself as a member of the infamous pirate's crew."

Hunter closed the book and stared down at the plain, unadorned cover. It had a faded red color, the color of dried blood. "It's amazing," he said. "A man escapes from a life of slavery, joins up with a crew of pirates, narrowly escapes with his life, then writes a book about the whole thing. I have to admit a certain admiration for a man like that. I'm surprised he was never recaptured as a runaway slave."

"His ex-master was fairly passive. He more than likely never reported it."

Hunter handed the book back to Summerfield, who gingerly handled it as if it were a Nuremburg Bible.

"Seems to me that we need to do something to stop this—whatever it is," Hunter said. "The problem is, any cop we try to tell this story to is going to think we're nuts. So, where do we go from here?"

Summerfield walked back to the bookcase and slid the volume into its place on the shelf, then turned to face Hunter.

"We go to Charleston."

"South Carolina?"

"Yep."

"Why Charleston?"

"There's someone there we need to talk to, someone who can shed light on this whole problem."

"Who is she?"

"She is a *he*, and you have to meet this person to believe he even exists. Let's just say he probably knows more about the subject of Death Defiers than just about anyone on the planet. Can you get away for a few days?"

Hunter shrugged his shoulders and leaned back in his chair. "I have some time off coming to me. I think I may be able to talk my editor into letting me go."

Then, he thought for a minute.

"You know, there is one person I think we should call, at least try to appraise her of the situation."

"Who?" Summerfield asked.

"Lisa."

Summerfield raised an eyebrow.

"Your ex-wife?" he asked.

"Not my ex-wife, *yet*. Anyway, she's been working hard on this case and I think she deserves to know that we may be on to something."

"You know she's going to think we're both nuts. Besides, all we have is conjecture at this point."

"Yeah, but I think she's bright enough to let the evidence speak for itself, no matter how impossible it may seem. Anyway, she may have evidence we don't know about, something that could help us."

Summerfield picked up the phone and dialed nine, then handed the receiver to Hunter.

"What's the number?" he asked.

John Aiden watched as the moon descended on the horizon of his estate in Williamsburg, Virginia, which was within earshot of the Golden Horseshoe Golf Club. Though Aiden was a member in good standing, he'd rarely played in recent years, having other things on his mind. But today he had decided to play nine holes.

Upon returning home, he stepped out of his Land Rover and appreciated the spectacular view. The moonlight reflected like a dream off the water of his private, well-stocked koi pond, golden fish swimming this way and that underneath the small, arched bridge upon which he now stood. He could hear the frogs calling to each other in the night, the screech of bats that would soon make a meal of them. All around him, the sounds of the swamp were beginning to come to life, but all Aiden could really focus on was the bone-white moonlight reflecting across the water.

He had been having a recurring dream the last few weeks, a dream he believed foretold the future. In his dream, Death, adorned in a billowing black shroud and carrying a large scythe, stood in a dense fog and knocked a skeletal hand upon his door. Suddenly, the scythe morphed into an old, rusty cutlass, and the shroud fell away to reveal a barnacle-encrusted skeleton minus its skull. When he opened the door, the specter reached out a hand and offered not death, but knowledge, the knowledge of a thousand lifetimes.

Upon waking, Aiden always thought that his sleeping vision was rather like Jesus in the wilderness being tempted by Satan, who offered all the kingdoms on Earth in return for obedience. But in the dream, when he reached out to take the hand, Aiden always awoke.

Suddenly, the frogs and bats stopped their serenade, and he looked around at the forest behind his house, wondering what could cause such profound stillness.

Then he heard something that startled him—glass breaking, the destructive sound of wood splintering.

He turned toward his house. Aiden lived alone and had never bothered to hire security guards to protect his collection, relying instead on electronic surveillance and alarm systems. But on this particular evening, Aiden had disarmed the system, knowing in some intuitive way he would have a visitor and what the visitor would be after. He had hoped, however, to allow its entrance without the use of excessive force.

Aiden ran to the house, a hundred yards away, saw that the front door—constructed of intricately carved heavy oak and stained glass—was smashed through and splintered as if it were a piece of rotted driftwood.

He cautiously stepped through the opening and peered around inside. Being rather timid and small, he realized long ago that he was no match for anyone larger than himself. That was why he had gotten a license for what he liked to think of as his equalizer, a nine-millimeter Glock he kept in a holster beneath his jacket and that he now held firmly in his hand.

Aiden listened. It sounded as if someone, or some *thing*, was in his office destroying the glass case that held his precious collection. Aiden felt a burning outrage, but knew he had to proceed carefully, so he swallowed back his rage.

He just *knew* this thing ransacking his office was supernatural. In some strange, telepathic way Aiden knew the personification of his recurring nightmare now lurked in his home office.

He glanced at the wooden floor leading to the carpeted hallway. Saw muddy tracks resembling misshapen, out-of-proportion footprints scattered willy-nilly.

Aiden crept quietly down the darkened hallway, listening to the sounds emanating from the last room on the left. On the floor in the hallway, the shadow of the intruder danced and jerked with odd movements, as if he was having some kind of seizure. Then, the shadow abruptly disappeared, followed by a loud *thump*.

Aiden stopped in his tracks and continued to listen. After several minutes of silence, he decided to take a chance.

"Hello, is anyone there?"

A bead of sweat trickled down his forehead and over his glasses. Everything remained quiet.

He tried again. "Hello, what's going on in there? I have a gun and I've called the police, so don't try anything."

Still no reaction or sound whatsoever. Aiden finally worked up the courage to stealthily move toward the office door, watching for telltale shadows cast by the single light from within the room.

Floorboards creaked beneath his feet.

He stood just outside the door and craned his neck to peek around the doorframe and inside. Lying in front of the glass case was a dark figure that Aiden could not quite make out. He glanced at the case itself and noticed one thing missing—the cup made from Blackbeard's skull.

Certain that the intruder was out cold, Aiden slipped the Glock back into its holster and walked carefully into the room, toward the heap on the floor.

Standing close to the body, he was able to plainly see the visitor, the culprit who had broken through his heavy oak door and smashed most of his prized collection to pieces.

Aiden stood gazing downward for several seconds, trying to comprehend the thing that lay at his feet, then turned as if to leave.

He took all of three steps before he fell to the floor in a dead faint.

Lisa listened to the message from Hunter for a third time, wondering if what she heard was real or some kind of practical joke. She would never put anything past Hunter when it came to practical joking, but she also knew that he took his job very seriously. And no matter how she tried to dismiss it, what he said actually made sense within the context of the present murder investigation.

The case was beginning to take on elements that frightened her, elements that were beyond rational explanation, and Lisa was not one to be easily frightened.

Hunter gave her the condensed version of recent events, beginning with the phone call from his friend at the museum, Jason Summerfield. He told her the bizarre story of Blackbeard's secret life, gruesome death, and possible rebirth. He also told her they would be going to Charleston to meet someone who could help them, but didn't say who it was or how they would help.

She turned off the machine and went to the bedroom to change from her uniform. As she thought about the message from Hunter, Lisa's mind wandered back to happier times, to the days when Hunter and she were together and expecting their first child—before life had come crashing down around them. Then followed the arguments, the endless nights of tears and anger, fighting over the least little thing. All she had wanted was Hunter to comfort her, to tell her everything would be okay, that losing the baby wasn't the end of the world.

But maybe she hadn't given Hunter the benefit of the doubt; after all, it was his baby, too. She should have tried harder to put herself in his shoes. It was likely that Hunter had been just as devastated as she, perhaps even more so, knowing what a traumatic experience it had been for his wife.

That's when she realized something, and it was like a slap in the face. She was still in love with Hunter. No escaping it, no denying it. It was time to face up to the facts and stop dancing around the truth. If something happened to Hunter, Lisa would be heartbroken, and she would never be able to live with herself.

She decided there was only one thing to do. She walked back into the living room, reached for the phone and picked it up to dial Hunter's number.

The doorbell rang at that precise moment.

Stanton sat upright in his chair like a schoolboy chided by his teacher for bad posture.

"I really need you here, Hunter," he said. "What's so important that you have to go all the way to Charleston, anyway? You know we don't have a travel budget to send you anywhere, especially out of state."

"Then I'll take a vacation. I have some time on the books."

"You want to work on vacation? I can't sanction that."

"You don't have to. We'll just say it's a vacation. If I happen to get a story, great. Besides, Edmondson can cover my beat while I'm gone, right?"

Stanton sighed deeply and shook his head.

"You know, if you weren't such a good reporter, I'd write you up for insubordination."

Hunter grinned. "But I *am* good. That's why you love me."

"You still haven't told me why you want to go to Charleston. Are you into something I should know about?"

"Maybe."

Stanton narrowed his eyes. "Don't play coy with me. I can tell when you're bullshitting me, and you are. Just give it to me straight. You're on to something with this swamp murder business, aren't you?"

"Maybe," was all Hunter would say.

"Look, if that's true, then just let the police handle it from here. It's not our job to stick our noses where they don't belong. And if I know you, that's exactly what you'll do."

"Okay, I'm on to something. But it's bigger, much bigger than just murder. If the things I'm hearing from my sources are true, it may be one of the biggest stories ever."

"What could be bigger than murder?"

"Just trust me on this. If I tried to explain it, you wouldn't believe me. Let's just say it's unlike anything we've ever written, probably any newspaper has ever written."

Stanton smirked. "Okay, be mysterious. But I'm telling you, you're officially on vacation, so don't try to come back later and charge me for overtime. It ain't gonna happen."

"Don't worry, I wouldn't think of it. I promise, you won't be sorry."

Stanton rolled his eyes and leaned back in his chair. "I should be so lucky."

Lisa laid the phone back in its cradle and put a hand on the butt of her service revolver. With all the killings that had been taking place lately, she was a little more on edge and a lot more cautious.

The knock on her door came a third time. She doubted if Hunter would be coming to her apartment this soon after she had seen him, though she couldn't discount the possibility. She also knew her parents or friends would call before coming over. That left either a salesman or a cop.

She slowly walked to her door and looked through the peephole. Outside stood a tall, well-muscled black man, someone she had never seen before. He looked rather anxious, but not in a bad way, just like he had something on his mind. He had a scar running down the side of his face that looked like he had been in a knife fight, and he was dressed in all black, but the clothes were casual, almost preppy.

"Who is it?" she called through the door.

She watched as the man stiffened and looked directly at the peephole.

"Officer Singleton? My name is Jefferson, Jonathan Jefferson. I'm here to talk to you about the murders in the swamp, and the death of my partner on Ocracoke Island."

Lisa tried to think. A death on Ocracoke Island? Then she remembered the story Hunter had written for the *Daily Tribune*. A diver from a research vessel off Ocracoke had decompressed too quickly on a dive and died from the bends. It was still under investigation.

Lisa unlocked the door, but kept the chain up. She opened the door slightly and peered out at the stranger through the crack.

"So how do I know you're not the killer?" she asked.

Jonathan looked annoyed at the question.

"Please. Do I look like a killer?"

Lisa eyed the scar on his neck.

Jonathan realized what she was looking at and smiled for the first time. "That's not what you think it is," he said, bringing his hand up to his neck. "It's from a shark attack, off the coast of Australia. Please, can we talk? I think I may have some important information that could help you crack this case."

"Why me?"

"Because, I've seen your name in the paper and you seem like a reasonable woman. Besides, some of what I have to say may sound a little strange."

Lisa eyed Jonathan up and down. "I'll bet."

Her face disappeared as she shut the door momentarily to take the chain off, then opened it back up. Lisa stood in the doorway, one hand still resting on her pistol.

Jonathan noticed the gun, then glanced back up at her.

"What, are you going to shoot me?"

Without missing a beat, Lisa said, "Maybe. It depends."

"On what?"

"On what you have to say."

She motioned him inside the apartment with a nod, then shut the door.

Jonathan looked around the apartment. Though it was small, it definitely had a woman's touch, with pastel drapes, a large vase of daisies on the coffee table, and what looked like several Picasso prints on the living room wall.

Lisa walked around a bar with three stools where a small TV sat on the counter.

"Would you like something to drink, Mr. Jefferson? I have coffee, soda, water, tea . . ."

"No thanks, I had something on the way here."

She reached up into one of the oak cabinets and grabbed a glass.

"Suit yourself. Have a seat."

Jonathan looked down at one of the stools, pulled it out,

then sat.

"Nice place you have here."

"Thanks. I like it."

After getting herself a glass of tea from the fridge, Lisa walked over to the bar and looked across at the man.

"So, what's this all about?"

Jonathan eyed her for a long minute, then blurted, "I think I know who the killer is."

Lisa carefully sat her glass on the counter and watched Jonathan for some sign of insincerity—a flinch of an eye, a bead of sweat—but saw none.

"So, who do you think the killer is?" she finally asked.

Jonathan put his elbows on the bar and steepled his fingers under his chin. "Before I answer that, let me ask you this. Have you ever heard of an old pirate ship called the *Adventure*?"

Lisa smirked at the question. "Of course. Who around here hasn't? It was the last known ship commanded by Edward Teach, or Thatch, or Blackbeard . . . or whatever you want to call him."

Jonathan raised his eyebrows, impressed with her answer. "I see you know your history. Well, people have been searching for the wreck for years, but no one has been able to find it." He rose from his seat and began pacing as he spoke. "I'm an underwater archeologist, and at home I started having this dream, the same one over and over, of a wrecked ship at the bottom of a sub-oceanic cave. I went over the dream in my mind again and again, trying to figure out what it meant, then one day it hit me. It had to be the *Adventure*."

Lisa furrowed her brow. "Why the *Adventure*?"

Jonathan stopped pacing. "Because, in the dream I could always look out the window of my boat's pilot house and see Ocracoke Island. I didn't know where the dream was coming from, or why I kept having the same one, but somehow I just knew it was right. It just *felt* right."

Lisa nodded and shot Jonathan a patronizing look. "Uh huh."

Jonathan stared down at the floor and shook his head, then glanced at her. "Look, I know this sounds crazy, but just hear me out."

Jonathan began pacing again and Lisa rolled her eyes.

"My partner, Dan Brickhouse, and I were searching the ocean floor not far from the Island in a place called Teach's Hole, which is where the *Adventure* was supposedly last seen. It's also where Blackbeard met his death."

"Did you say Brickhouse?" Lisa interrupted.

"Have you heard of him?"

Lisa nodded. "Yeah. Wasn't he the one killed in that diving accident off Ocracoke a couple of weeks ago?"

Jonathan turned his eyes away, a painful expression on his face. "He was. But it was no accident."

"Oh? I thought the sheriff said he surfaced too fast on a dive and got the bends."

"That's what the sheriff said. But he wasn't there when it happened. I was."

Lisa said nothing.

"I pulled him up out of the water. Before too long, he went into convulsions and . . . well, you know the rest."

Jonathan resumed his pacing. "With a remote-control robotic camera we found the wreck of the *Adventure* exactly where my dream predicted it would be—at the bottom of a sub-oceanic cave, which is why no one had been able to find it before. The cave opening was barely bigger than the ship itself. Inside the wreck of the ship, we found a secret compartment in the captain's quarters that was partially rotted away, and within the compartment was an old wine bottle that contained what we thought was a map. But it wasn't a map."

Jonathan abruptly stopped and turned to Lisa, making her flinch.

"I wish you'd quit doing that," she said.

"What we did find in the bottle was an ancient animal skin, older than the ship itself, with some writing on it that looked like Latin, but I know it wasn't Latin. It was some kind of hybrid language, like a code. I took a photo of it and e-mailed it to a friend of mine at a museum in Raleigh to get it translated. I'm not sure what happened to that e-mail, but I believe that whatever was written on that skin has something to do with these murders."

Jonathan's stare became more intense, making Lisa uneasy. Hidden behind the kitchen bar, she slowly put a hand on the butt of her pistol.

"I believe it contained a spell."

Lisa showed her surprise. "A spell? What kind of spell?"

"A spell to raise the dead," Jonathan said.

Lisa stood stock still, not breathing, thinking of what to do next. Put him under arrest? She could say he was breaking and entering, but she had let him in herself. She could just say that he suddenly went crazy. After all, she was a cop and it was his word against hers.

Jonathan's gaze softened. "I know how all this sounds. Believe me. I'm a scientist; I deal with facts. But if you had seen what I've seen, you wouldn't think it was so far-fetched."

Though Lisa was leery of the man standing across from her kitchen bar, she was also curious. "What exactly did you see?"

Jonathan's eyes became distant, haunted somehow.

"When Dan was still on the bottom, he worked close to the cave, near the edge, looking for anything that might have detached itself from the wreck on its way down. Then, he said he saw something move under the sand and thought it might be a crab or a flounder. But it wasn't. It was something that scared the shit out of him, so much so that he immediately started hyperventilating and then just started talking gibberish. He began his ascent, but was in too big of a hurry."

He gazed down at the apartment floor as if he could see his partner engulfed in the murky darkness of the Atlantic, trying to make his way to the surface. "I yelled at him to slow down, to decompress, but he just kept ascending and hyperventilating and talking nonsense. There was nothing I could do to stop him. I ran over to the side of the boat, and watched him bob up in the water, frantic with fear, trying to grab the ladder to hoist himself out of the water."

The man looked up at Lisa. She was beginning to think there might be something to what he said, some kind of twisted truth. She softened her expression, encouraging Jonathan to finish the story.

"I helped him up the ladder onto the dive platform. I could tell he was already pretty bad off. He seemed confused, as if he wasn't sure where he was. I got his mask and tank off, and he kind of fell back on the deck and just lay there. Then he suddenly grabbed me by the collar and pulled me right down in front of his face. He looked like he was close to insanity. His eyes were wild and unfocused. I've never seen anyone so terrified." Jonathan turned and walked slowly back toward the living room in silence.

"So, what did he say?" Lisa asked.

Jonathan took a deep breath, hesitating, as though he didn't want to dredge up the memory of his friend's last moments. He licked his lips and ran a hand over his black, curly hair, then spun back around and faced Lisa from across the room, trying his best to maintain his composure.

"He said, 'The bones, Jon, the bones. They're *alive*.'"

John Aiden woke up sprawled in the middle of his exhibit room. He felt like he had gone on a bender. A large goose egg throbbed on the side of his forehead. When he had fainted, he fell head-first onto the floor and now had a headache the size of the Dismal Swamp. His limbs ached as if he had just lost a wrestling match, and he had to struggle to force himself to move.

Propping himself up on one elbow, he reached for his glasses, which had fallen off but remained miraculously intact. Aiden slipped them on and looked around the room, his eyes coming to rest on a heap lying at his feet, remembering it as the reason he had fainted in the first place.

Cautiously, he sat up and tried to stand, but found it difficult. His legs wobbled like those of a newborn deer. His headache felt like someone was working over his brain with a jackhammer. He reached up and felt the fleshy, raised knob on the side of his head, wincing at the pain.

Aiden studied the figure on the floor, then noticed his Glock lying nearby. He reached down to pick it up and nearly fell, but managed to keep his balance and retrieve the gun. It made him feel safer, felt good in his hand, but he doubted it would be effective against the thing on the floor.

Suddenly the shape made some kind of movement, like it was trying to catch its breath. It was turned on its side, away from him, but he was afraid to touch it. Instead, he walked around to the other side.

Immediately, he was sorry he had done so.

It was a skeleton. And it seemed to be alive.

The being was encrusted with sea barnacles and looked as if it had been underwater for eons. The large chalice that had been fashioned from the skull of Blackbeard and removed from Aiden's display case now seemed to be attached to the rest of the skeleton, and growing its own bone mass at an astonishing rate.

More amazing were the visible signs of muscle tissue beginning to form and attach itself, ligament-by-ligament to the bones. It reminded him of an intertwined mass of huge, rapidly-moving slugs, stretching with every evolution, then coming to rest as each one found its mark and anchored itself to the bone. It was like watching a body decay in reverse. The green encrustation was starting to dry and turn to dust, flaking off the bones like old paint and falling to the floor. It was as if the thing was growing a new body.

Though he wanted to, Aiden didn't move. *Couldn't* move. He simply watched as cell upon cell, muscle upon muscle, vein upon vein, formed and linked to other cells, muscles, and veins. Internal organs grew at such speed it made Aiden think of the time-lapse films he had seen in school of flowers opening and closing, or snails making their way across a landscape like sprinters in an Olympic race. The facial bones, which had grown from the chalice itself, were now covered with muscle of their own. Skin was starting to form, covering the muscle and veins underneath like an ocean tide creeping over a sandy beach.

The power this being possessed was beyond anything mankind had seen since the days of Jesus Christ Himself. But Aiden knew this was far from the work of Christ, and far from the hand of God. He was sure, in fact, that it was just the opposite.

And what's more, he wanted to be a part of it.

Lisa stared at her guest for several silent minutes, letting his story sink in. She wondered just how crazy Jonathan Jefferson was. His partner had said the bones were alive, but of course Lisa knew that was impossible. Bones don't just come to life on their own, do they?

She thought about Hunter's phone call, and her own nightmare the night before. She felt like she needed to hear the words again, just to be sure she hadn't imagined them.

"He said the bones were alive?"

Jonathan nodded slowly, his eyes like two pools of black water, somber and haunted.

"So, what happened next?"

Jonathan's mind seemed to return from somewhere far away. He focused his eyes on Lisa. "Well, then he just lay back down and eventually started convulsing. I took the boat back to the island, called the Coast Guard on my radio and told them what had happened. But by the time I got there . . ." Jonathan's voice trailed off.

Lisa felt a knot in the pit of her stomach. To lose a friend is a horrible experience to have to live through, especially when that friend practically dies in your arms, and you know there's nothing you, or anyone, can do. "I'm sorry," she whispered.

Jonathan attempted a smile, but the experience of the last two weeks weighed him down. "It's okay. I haven't even had time to really think about it much." He let out a heavy breath. "We spent a lot of years together, Dan and me. We bought that boat and chased our dream of finding sunken wrecks like two school kids following a pirate's treasure map. When we found the *Adventure*, we thought we had made our fortune. It was incredible to see it on that monitor. And then to go down and actually witness it firsthand was . . . well, the experience was beyond words." His eyes seemed to glow as he spoke, but then the darkness returned as he said, "Then, to have this happen."

Questions started to form in Lisa's mind, the cop in her overriding the emotion of her sympathy toward Jonathan.

"If your friend had decompression sickness, couldn't he have been hallucinating?"

Jonathan stopped pacing and turned. "He could have, but remember, the reason Dan surfaced in the first place was because something had terrified him. To the point that he ignored his years of dive training. He saw something down there, and I think what he saw was something that had become reanimated, something that was alive that shouldn't have been. It was just too much for his mind to handle."

For the sake of argument Lisa decided to throw rationality out the window. "You said you knew who the killer was. Do you think Blackbeard the Pirate came to life down there and is now walking around killing people? Kind of like Blackbeard's Ghost, right?"

Jonathan casually walked back to the bar and took a seat. He crossed his arms on the bar and looked at Lisa, said, "What do you know about Blackbeard? I mean the real Blackbeard, not the fairy tale version."

She turned and walked slowly towards the refrigerator, her back to the man, considering the question, then stopped and spun around. "I just know that he lived in the late 17th and early 18th centuries, and that he was greatly feared by sailors and merchants all along the east coast and even into the Caribbean. I also know that he was supposed to be in league with the devil."

Jonathan smiled. "Aha! You just hit the nail on the head. He was *supposed* to be in league with the devil. But there is no supposition about it. He definitely was, and what's more, that devil continued to occupy those bones even after the pirate's death."

Lisa shook her head in disbelief. "Look, Mr. Jefferson—"

"*Jonathan*, please."

"Jonathan," she continued, "you're a nice guy and I'm sure you mean well, but—"

Jonathan cut her off. "Have you ever heard of Diablero or the Death Defier?"

Lisa's heart rate suddenly jumped. She felt herself getting flushed as she recalled Hunter's words on her answering machine.

"How about Obeah?" Jonathan continued.

"Go on," she said quietly.

Jonathan seemed to study Lisa as he told the story. "In Sonoran Indian lore, the Death Defier is a human that can cheat death and has the ability to transform into any kind of animal—a bird, a coyote, a wolf, *anything*. He must also feed off of the living in order to maintain his energy. Basically, he feeds on their—on *our*—souls."

Lisa eyed Jonathan. "How does he do that?"

Jonathan shrugged. "I don't know. He just does it. He beheads the victim and captures their soul somehow, then that person becomes a part of the creature as he absorbs their life experience, their knowledge, their memories, everything about them."

Lisa was horrified to think of people suffering through such an experience. How would it be to look out at the world through the eyes of a monster, knowing there was nothing you could do to stop it and no possibility of escape?

It would be Hell on Earth.

She shuddered. "How do you know all this, anyway?"

Jonathan smiled ever so slightly, as if hiding the world's biggest secret. "I have inside information."

Lisa narrowed her eyes and took a drink of tea. "What kind of inside information?"

"I know someone who knows something about what's going on. In fact, you could say he wrote the book on the subject."

"And who would that be?"

"Someone I've known for a long time. Someone I've known my whole life, in fact."

Lisa was growing frustrated, tired of playing games with this man. She wanted answers. "Okay, you said you knew who the killer was. Why don't you enlighten me on that?"

Jonathan frowned. "You mean you haven't figured it out, yet?"

"Hey, you came to me, remember?" Lisa said, getting pissed off at the rambling nature of this conversation. "Stop playing games and just spit it out. You think the bones of Blackbeard the Pirate are walking around killing people because he's some kind of reincarnated Diablero or whatever. Right?"

He held up his hands in resignation. "Hey, you said it, not me."

But Lisa wasn't giving in that easily. "But that's what you meant, wasn't it? Edward Teach is alive and well and on his way to Virginia."

Jonathan nodded slowly. "That about sums it up, yep."

Lisa wasn't sure if she had just been victorious or if she was just being conned. But her gut told her, like it or not, the man sitting in front of her was not crazy and could be trusted. And her gut instinct was rarely wrong. The fact that everything Jonathan had said seemed in line with the message from Hunter didn't hurt his case, either.

"So what's your plan?" she said.

Jonathan's eyes brightened. "Well, first, we go to Charleston, South Carolina."

Lisa felt like she had just been punched in the gut. "Did you say Charleston?"

"Yeah, why?"

Lisa's mouth hung open for a few seconds before she

answered. "Nothing, it's just that . . . ." she trailed off, thinking of Hunter and wondering exactly what it was he had gotten himself into.

John Aiden sat against a wall on the hardwood floor of his exhibit room, knees pulled up to his chin, watching the transformation before him play itself out. He could see no more signs of growth, but thought that perhaps there may still be something happening internally.

As he had this last thought, however, the creature began to stir. A moan escaped its mouth, and Aiden froze with fear. Long, jet-black hair cascaded down onto the floor, obscuring the face from view, and he could just make out a beard of the same color sprouting from the chin.

While Aiden watched, the head lifted slowly from the floor. The being sat upright, much in the same position Aiden had been. They stared at each other in apprehension. Its face was quite handsome, reminding Aiden of Errol Flynn, the old movie star, with a long, black beard. The eyes, however, green as the cold, bottomless north Atlantic, filled him with terror. They held no sign of bewilderment or confusion, as they should have after such an ordeal, but rather were clear and focused on a purpose that Aiden could not begin to fathom. Looking into those eyes, he felt as though an eternity of knowledge and wisdom lay within. The man seemed to be sizing Aiden up as if to decide whether he were of any value.

Faster than Aiden could have imagined, the man morphed into a giant wolf-like creature, at least a hundred pounds heavier than the largest bear Aiden had ever seen.

He had no time to react as the thing grabbed Aiden by his throat in a clawed hand and hoisted him off his feet. A snout smelling of rotted flesh breathed into his face. He felt his pants become wet in the crotch as he struggled to breathe. Aiden clutched at the immense, hairy appendage that held him, but it was like steel, solid and unyielding. He stopped struggling and tried desperately to communicate as the beast turned its heavy head slowly from side to side, like a dog inspecting its prey before devouring it. Rows of razor-sharp teeth glistened and dripped saliva. A deep-throated rumble came from within its huge body, warning of impending attack.

Instead of attacking him, however, the beast's grip released ever so slightly, allowing Aiden a gasp of air. His feet continued to dangle above the floor by at least a foot.

Then, the thing spoke in a throaty, deep rasp that Aiden thought could only be the voice of a demon. "Speak," it said.

Momentarily taken aback by the thing's speech, Aiden took a breath of stinking air and tried to choose his words carefully. To say the wrong thing could mean anything from decapitation to disembowelment, neither of which sounded pleasant. Finally he croaked, "I . . . I," he said with a strangled voice. The grip loosened a bit more. "I can help you," he finally managed to say.

"You?" the thing snarled. "How can you help me?"

"I . . . I have . . . boat . . ." was all Aiden could get out before he began to slip into unconsciousness.

The vise-grip around his neck suddenly loosened, and Aiden, caught off guard, fell to the ground, sprawled out like a child who had just fallen off his bicycle. He looked up from the floor, expecting to see the wolf-creature staring back with feral, red-rimmed eyes, but instead saw the man who had been there before, hair hanging in black strands around his black-bearded face. Aiden felt relieved, rubbing his neck with a hand, trying to get some feeling back.

The man stared down at him, like a lion eyeing a lamb. "Where is this boat?" the stranger asked.

"It's at my dock, in the marina. I can take you there, take you wherever you want to go," he said.

"Help me, and you'll be rich and powerful beyond your wildest dreams."

Aiden could not believe the stark contrast between the snarling wolf-thing and this seemingly docile, almost humble man. He didn't know what exactly the man's mission was, but he knew he had come too far to back off now.

And being rich and powerful sounded pretty damned good.

"You can count on me," was all Aiden could say.

The giant steel suspension cables of the Cooper River Bridge became visible from the highway against a bright blue sky as Hunter and Summerfield approached Charleston, South Carolina. Though Hunter had developed a healthy respect for heights, his wasn't a phobia. He had always enjoyed looking down at the world from bridges and skyscrapers, seeing life from a wider perspective.

As they got closer, he glanced over at Summerfield. "Sure you don't want me to drive? You look a little peaked."

Summerfield smirked. "I've driven over this bridge plenty of times. It's scary only when the wind's blowing."

They came to the foot of the bridge and began their ascent, and as if to substantiate Summerfield's statement, the bridge did indeed seem to sway, if only slightly.

"Yeah," Hunter said dryly, "I see what you mean."

As they came to the center of the bridge, Hunter could see pleasure boats and tankers making their way in and out of Charleston Harbor. The salt sea mixing with diesel fumes and car exhaust made for an interesting smell, but one which Hunter didn't much care for.

As he considered why he was there and what they were about to do, Hunter's thoughts turned to Lisa. He wondered if she had received his message and what she would do about it. She probably figured he was crazy. But she knew he wasn't prone to making up fairy tales and ghost stories.

He found himself wishing she was next to him in the seat of Summerfield's Prius instead of Summerfield.

"You know," Summerfield said, snapping Hunter out of his daydream, "it's kind of ironic that we're headed to

Charleston of all places. Remember, this is where Blackbeard held his blockade. But after weeks of pillaging ships coming in and out of the harbor, he demanded nothing more than a chest of medicine from the city itself. Then, he took that and all his ill-gotten gains, and left the harbor without ever firing a shot or harming a soul. Yet the city of Charleston was in mortal fear of this man. Kind of makes you wonder just how charismatic the guy really was."

Hunter stared straight ahead as the Prius coasted down the far side of the bridge and into Charleston.

"Yeah, or maybe he was just crazy."

"Ha! Crazy like a fox."

"Seems to me that Blackbeard had a lot going for him if he would have changed his ways and took the offer Governor Eden made him—to swear off piracy. But he just couldn't seem to leave it alone. He just had to be a pirate. It was in his blood. He was like a man . . ."

Summerfield looked at him. "Like a man *possessed?*"

Hunter nodded. "Yeah, like a man possessed."

Summerfield smiled. "I guess it's true what they say about fact being stranger than fiction."

Hunter continued to think about the ramifications of a demon-possessed soul. He had always believed in God, ever since he was a child, though there had been times in his life he had questioned his faith. Especially when God had apparently decided that the life of his unborn child and his marriage were expendable. But Hunter soon realized that in times like those, faith was the only thread connecting him to what he hoped was a benign and merciful God, one that would help him piece his life back together.

But the reality of the situation he now found himself in far outweighed any kind of trouble he thought he may be having in his life. This was something unimaginably evil, something that had to be stopped. The big question was, of course, how do you stop the unstoppable? And if there was ever a time Hunter would need his faith, he knew it would be coming very soon.

The old man took another sip of tea, watching from his front-porch swing as the sunlight crawled across his lawn, slowly feeding on the shadow of his house, chipping away inch by inch. He never wore sunglasses because he felt they detracted from the beauty of natural color. He loved the light, loved to bask in the warmth of the summer sun, watch its beams cascade through the windows of his old house in the afternoon, dust mites swirling through them like a fine mist. The sun had deepened his dark complexion over the years, made the wrinkles around his eyes multiply like the tributaries of a great river. But he didn't mind. The fact that he had spent so much of his life in darkness made his appreciation of the light even more profound.

As the old man thought of this, he considered how his life was about to change, maybe for the better, maybe not. But it was about to change. Soon, people would come and ask him many questions, some he could answer, other answers they would have to discover for themselves.

And *he* will come, too.

The old man shuddered at this thought, took another drink of green tea. A marvelous thing, green tea, he thought. The Chinese were a brilliant and resourceful people, surviving the centuries as a race, much like his own people, who spent their lives in the jungles and plains of darkest Africa.

Then came the slave traders and the white men, and life had never been the same. Even so, he was thankful to be in America, despite its flaws.

But there were some things he had found hard to let go, things that had been ingrained in him by his parents and their parents before them. They had brought these things with them to this country and now they haunted him, tortured him, refused to let go, demanded that he do their bidding.

As if on cue, his mind suddenly shifted to a vision of the horizon, with water below and sky above. The cup and saucer slipped from his trembling hands and crashed to the floor, its precious contents seeping through the cracks between the wooden slats. As he watched, his eyes seemed as if they were blind, staring into black, empty space, but the opposite was true. He was seeing what *it* was seeing, what *it* wanted him to see. *It* wanted him to know that *it* was coming, and was now very close.

It, or he, was on a boat of some kind. He could see a teakwood rail and a brass bell. There was a cabin with windows and he could hear the thrum of the engines as they plowed through the water toward their destination. Someone else was there. A thin, short man with glasses was driving the boat and saying something he could not understand. He could feel the wind blowing on his face and feel the fine spray of salt water as it leapt over the bow, could smell the salty sea air.

The vision lasted a few more seconds and then, like waking from a dream, the old man returned to his senses and sunk down in the porch swing, drained.

Not much longer now, he knew, and his destiny, perhaps even his death, would be upon him.

The man once known as Edward Teach felt the presence of the old man inside his head as he looked out over the vast expanse of the Atlantic. The salt sea breeze blew through his black mane, cooling his sunburned skin. Though he knew the old man was not afraid of death, he could still feel the awe, the sense of foreboding that was there. Teach would allow him to see many things, to witness the terrifying power he possessed. It would be enough to let him know who held the reins and controlled their intertwined destiny, a destiny that lay within a book of secrets that only the old man, the shaman, could unlock.

Many of the things The Teacher had accumulated over the centuries in the body of the old man he had once possessed had been lost and forgotten when Teach destroyed him. The Death Defier had been forced to start over again and he had lost the knowledge gained from reading the ancient book, one he had taken part in writing. But before The Teacher had died, he had taught his apprentice many things.

Now, the old man held the secrets inside that ancient mind, a mind full of puzzles and riddles that even this demon would find difficult to unravel. But Teach could be very persuasive and was confident that the old shaman would come through in the end. He would have no choice.

Teach absentmindedly ran his hands over the strange clothing he now wore, things that the human, John Aiden, had purchased for him. Something called slacks, a shirt made of strange fabric. Even the shoes were unusual, not stiff, uncomfortable leather like the ones he had worn when he last walked the Earth. He liked the things called sunglasses, for it blocked the intense light of the morning sun and kept his eyes hidden from others.

His long black hair and beard would have given him an almost Middle East appearance, were it not for his white skin, now red from the sun. He had not bothered to braid his hair or his beard, but thought that he may do so at a later date. In the past it had served to make him appear more formidable, though he was already supremely confident in his ability to cause fear.

As a man, Blackbeard had been a force to reckon with, a pirate in every sense of the word, taking whatever his heart desired and leaving death and destruction in his wake. Yet even though his soul was full of wanton lust for riches and a need for power, he was a pragmatic man, methodical in his approach and conquest of ships of the sea. He knew what he wanted, but took it only when he felt he was fully prepared to do what was necessary to obtain it.

Teach was also a highly intelligent man, conversant in several languages and able to read and write. In fact, he kept a log of many of his journeys and conquests, though most of them had been lost over the centuries, buried at the bottom of the Atlantic with the *Adventure* or confiscated by the Royal Navy, who likely filed them away in some vast warehouse, never to be seen again. Communication was of utmost importance when relaying to prisoners exactly what was expected of them, and exactly how they would meet their death if they did not comply with your wishes. Teach was an excellent communicator, and therefore became a feared and infamous pirate.

When The Teacher came, Blackbeard was leery, but drawn to him by the mystique and by curiosity. The power The Teacher possessed was beyond anything Blackbeard or the other pirates had ever encountered. Meeting in the dark, under cover of the night, in the swamp or aboard their vessels, they learned things long forgotten, and saw things that were both astounding and terrifying. The Teacher moved cypress trees and plants and even huge boulders with his mind. Sometimes The Teacher would change into a wolf-like creature or a bear. Or he would reanimate the dead, make corpses rise and walk again. Many of the pirates fled in terror at this, never to return. But Blackbeard refused to run, for he feared no man, living or dead.

And then, there were the sacrifices for The Teacher, prolonging his life throughout the centuries with their blood. Many, many sacrifices. People in Elizabeth Town and Bath began asking questions, but no one had managed to uncover the nightmarish truth.

As the months rolled by, Blackbeard decided that being the student was not enough. He wanted more. *He* wanted to be The Teacher; to be the Death Defier. So he caught The Teacher off guard and cleanly lopped off his head with his cutlass. The demon came into him almost immediately, and Blackbeard, perhaps for the first time in his life, understood the true meaning of evil, and the true meaning of fear.

The demon eventually became too strong and Blackbeard found he was no longer in control.

Teach thought back to the day, nearly three centuries ago, when he lay flat on his back on the wooden deck of the English Navy ship as his life's blood gushed from him, staring up as Captain Maynard gazed down at him with unbelieving eyes. Only moments before, a crewman had struck Blackbeard with a sword and nearly severed his head. That was when he—the demon—had revived and discovered he was alone in the body. Up until that time, it had always been a struggle, fighting against the humanity and the morality that even Blackbeard seemed to possess.

But unlike Blackbeard, there were no accommodating souls aboard the Navy ship into which the demon could pass. He was trapped, doomed to inhabit a lifeless body indefinitely, perhaps forever.

Fortunately, the crew never destroyed the head, as they should have.

Then, the man with the dark soul had come and reawakened him, reenergized him, allowed him to once again walk the Earth, to find and reattach his missing skull.

And to grow a new body.

The demon smiled at this, knowing that a new body was but the beginning of bigger and better things to come.

Blackbeard glanced at Aiden, thinking he would eventually kill the man. But he still had some usefulness. Aiden seemed dedicated, yet was nothing more than an opportunist, trying to save his own skin. Aiden's ancestors had once turned tail and run away from him and the other pirates infesting North Carolina, hiding like a bunch of cowards in the colony in Virginia. Teach would take great pleasure in disemboweling him, perhaps even hold up an intestine to let him get a look before he collapsed to the ground.

The demon turned and surveyed the boat, a marvel of engineering. Sleek and quick, without the use of sails. Instead, the vessel employed what was known as diesel power, twin turbine-combustion engines that pushed it through the water by way of turbo propellers. Aiden had explained the entire workings of the boat to Teach, and of course, he understood it completely. He found that he was able to comprehend many things, and astonishingly fast. Being a demon with supernatural powers had its advantages.

He would learn as much as he could about this new world and about this culture. America and the world had changed dramatically in the last three centuries, but some reading, watching, and listening would quickly fill the gaps in his knowledge. And by doing this, he would also learn its weaknesses and exploit them.

Teach thought about the irony of his name, and that he, indeed, was a teacher. And he thought about the things all people of the Earth would soon learn from him.

Hunter reflected on the times he and Lisa had visited what the locals called the Low Country as he and Summerfield drove through the streets of Charleston. He eyed a Starbucks and remembered how they had sat beside that very window and watched as the many bicyclists pedaled by, soaking up the sun of a bright summer's day, narrowly avoiding crashing into one another. He remembered how they had ridden their own bikes in a local park and how he had nearly fallen into a waterway that ran the length of the park.

Lisa had purchased a handmade basket at one of the shops on Market Street. They had stood for half an hour, watching in amazement as an old woman weaved the basket, nimble fingers moving like an accomplished violinist, the strands of sweetgrass intertwining like intimate lovers. After she finished, Lisa thanked the woman, paid her, and inspected the basket as if it were a Monet.

They rode their bikes downtown and all along Battery Street, down Concord Street to Waterfront Park, getting wet in the sprinklers, laughing as they cruised down the sidewalk past rows of live oak trees. They ended the night at one of the local clubs, drinking beer and listening to the sounds of a cover band playing tunes too old for either of them to remember, but they enjoyed it just the same. They talked of the past and the future and discussed what they would name their baby and what kind of diapers they should buy.

The bed and breakfast they had stayed in was quaint, and quite a bit cheaper than the hotels. There, they enjoyed the company of the other guests, some from as far away as Alaska, and drank sherry and ate homemade cornbread. At night they made love in the antique bed, enjoying each other's bodies as if they had just met, basking in the afterglow and wondering what tomorrow would bring.

Hunter felt a tear begin to form, glanced sideways at Summerfield to make sure he wasn't looking, then wiped it away with the side of his finger.

Had he really been foolish enough to let her get away, to cast aside years of a carefully cultivated relationship because of his own pride? The baby's death was certainly beyond anything either of them could control, but his reaction to it was not. Retreating, hiding in the dark recesses of his own emotions, shutting out the one who needed him most, who he needed most—that should have been preventable, *was* preventable. And Hunter swore if he could have just one more chance to prove himself, to show he had learned his lesson and learned it well, he would never again lose sight of what mattered most—his Lisa.

"There's the house up ahead." Summerfield pointed with a long finger at a plain-looking white house with a single dormer window jutting from a wooden-shingled roof, and a covered front porch with a swing that hung from two chains. In the swing sat an old black man of about 75 or 80, staring solemnly ahead, lost in thought, perhaps. He was dressed in khaki pants and a red button-down shirt, with dusty, black shoes.

They parked by the curb and Hunter saw an old powder-blue Buick Skylark sitting in the narrow driveway. The man on the porch didn't seem to notice them. They both got out of the car and Hunter followed as Summerfield led the way.

They walked up the creaky porch steps. As they ascended the steps, Hunter noticed a broken tea cup lying in front of the swing, amidst a small pool of tea that glistened in the sun. He then looked at the old man. He was clean shaven, his short black hair graying on the sides. The man appeared younger than he had from a distance. He was still lost in thought, and Hunter wondered what the man was thinking about.

Suddenly, the old man's eyes fixed on them, and Hunter felt a small twinge of anxiety, unprepared for the intense scrutiny. Then, the man smiled, and Hunter felt a little more at ease.

"Ah, Mr. Summerfield, and Mr.—ah, Mr. Singleton, correct?"

The old man's voice was gravelly and deep, but the accent was unusual, an odd mix of African and southern U.S., and Hunter wondered where the man could be from.

Summerfield and the old man shook hands and the man stood. He was tall, maybe six-one or six-two, and solid, like a wrestler or a football player. Hunter was certain the man could hold his own in a fight.

Summerfield smiled and glanced at Hunter.

"Hunter, I'd like you to meet the one man who knows more about Blackbeard the pirate than anyone alive."

Hunter stepped forward and took the man's hand. Instantly, he had the strangest feeling, as if unseen fingers were probing the recesses of his mind, searching its shadows. But Hunter merely attributed this to stress and lack of sleep.

Summerfield said, "This, Hunter, is my old friend and partner in crime, Mr. Caesar Jefferson."

Caesar greeted him with a wide grin.

Hunter's mouth suddenly went dry.

As they stood inside Caesar's house, Hunter looked in awe at the photos and paintings adorning the white plaster walls. Images of life at sea, of fishing villages and of men as salty as Barnacle Bill the sailor. He could see that Caesar himself was in most of the photos, surrounded by men posing with fish they had caught, some small, and a few sharks so large they had to be held up by cranes with steel cables.

Caesar made a sweeping gesture with his hand. "This is my humble abode, and I hope you'll feel free to make it your own. My house is also your house."

The house smelled like salty sea air. Hunter stared at bookshelves crammed with volumes by Mark Twain, W.E.B. DuBois, Harriet Beecher Stowe, and Washington Irving. The bookshelves were constructed of plywood and bricks, as if Caesar had built them himself. Hunter couldn't see a television anywhere.

As he drew his attention back to the photos, Hunter noticed some of them were daguerreotypes, an early type of photograph developed in the late 1830s. More interesting, however, was that Caesar—or a family member with an extremely strong resemblance—also seemed to be present in those photos, likely a father or grandfather. As they were led into the kitchen, he made a mental note to ask about it later.

The kitchen was cramped, with a table shoved up against one wall and surrounded by three chairs. The chairs resembled padded seats from a greasy-spoon diner, complete with sparkling silver plastic covers.

Caesar turned and smiled at them. "What would you gentlemen care to drink? I have green tea, and water, but not much else, I'm afraid. As you can see, I live by humble means."

Hunter answered first. "Green tea is fine. I drink it pretty often, myself."

Summerfield looked at Hunter and smirked.

"What?"

"Since when do you like green tea?"

Hunter smiled. "Hey, I'm not a complete Neanderthal, okay?"

After filling three tea cups and sitting down at the kitchen table, Summerfield took a sip of his drink, then eyed the old man. To Hunter, Summerfield had the look of a reporter preparing for an interview.

"Caesar, I've known you for many years," Jason Summerfield said, "and I know that you have special gifts. I know there are certain things you can see, things you can sense that no one else can. You know why we're here, what we're looking for. Is there anything you can tell us about the demon—the Obeah—and Blackbeard?"

The old man stared at Summerfield for a moment, then at Hunter, whose heart began racing at the mention of Blackbeard's name. He was still having trouble accepting as fact a three-hundred-year-old pirate walking the Earth in the twenty-first century.

"I will tell you what you want to know. But first, you must understand what it is you are asking."

The two men waited, expecting Caesar to continue.

Instead, he took another sip of tea before saying, "You are asking me to be a cackler."

Hunter was bewildered. "I'm sorry. A what?"

Summerfield said to Hunter, "It's an old pirate term. It means someone who gives away secrets, someone who can't keep their mouth shut." He turned back to the old man. "There are lives at stake. Many have died, and many more may die if we don't put a stop to this, and soon."

Caesar looked down at the tabletop and sighed, then seemed to make up his mind.

"Yes, it is him, it is Blackbeard. But that which resides in him is no longer human. The Obeah has taken over completely, and it means to recover the book, the one in which is written the ancient and forgotten rituals, which Blackbeard hid, expecting he would return one day. He has returned, and the book still awaits."

Hunter could feel the dread building inside him. "What exactly is in this book?"

"Spells, gathered from all parts of the world. Spells that could make him powerful, so powerful that no mortal man could ever destroy him. But the cost of casting these spells was so great that Blackbeard, in his human form, was not willing to pay the price. However, the demon that possesses Edward Teach does not care about paying prices. That is why he is coming for me."

Hunter couldn't hide his surprise. "Why does he need you?"

"Because I was a shaman, one who practices Vodun, or *Voodoo* as most in America know it. I studied under The Teacher and learned things even Blackbeard did not know. Blackbeard the human was simply a vessel for a power he did not understand."

"How do you know so much about the book and Blackbeard?" Hunter asked.

Summerfield and Caesar shared a conspiratorial glance, then looked at Hunter. Caesar spoke, "Have you not yet realized who I am?"

Hunter could feel the cobwebs slowly clearing. Not possible, he thought, yet he knew it was true—this was *the* Caesar Jefferson, alive and well after more than three centuries. At least now the old daguerreotypes hanging on Caesar's wall made sense. It was Caesar who appeared in each one, not distant ancestors.

Lisa and Jonathan rode in silence for much of the way, speaking only perfunctorily. Jonathan's Land Rover was a far cry from her old Subaru, the comfort level well above average. The soft Wynton Marsalis tunes emanating from his CD player could have easily put her to sleep under other circumstances.

She still wasn't able to trust Jonathan, at least not completely. She wasn't convinced that everything he said was the God's honest truth, or that he had even *told* her everything. But her instincts told her it was right. She just prayed that Jonathan Jefferson knew what he was doing. She chanced a sideways glance at him, thinking fleetingly about pulling her pistol and making him turn the truck around, but decided against it.

Her thoughts turned to Hunter and Summerfield. More than likely, they were probably up to their necks in trouble. She and Jonathan had discussed calling the sheriff to tell him about their hunch, but the more they thought about it, the more they realized if *they* thought the whole thing was crazy, the sheriff was likely to think even worse.

Instead, Lisa called her father, Liang, who would at least listen without interrupting. And as a retired detective, he could also give her some advice. As her luck would have it, she got her father's voicemail instead, so Lisa gave him the short version of the facts. It had taken two phone calls to get the entire message through, but she managed to fill Liang in on what Hunter and Summerfield had surmised, and that they were going to Charleston.

Farmland gave way to dense forest. Far above the trees the clouds began to turn dark shades of pink and red with the approaching twilight.

Lisa decided it was time for some answers. "Tell me again why we're going to Charleston," she said. "Are we going there to see someone?"

"That's a pretty good guess."

"Does this someone happen to know something about Edward Teach?"

Jonathan's hooded eyes showed surprise. "How did you know that? Is there something you aren't telling me?"

Lisa looked at the road ahead and let out a sigh. "My husband called just before you came and told me that he and a friend of ours—Jason Summerfield—were going to Charleston to find an old man who knows more about Blackbeard than anyone alive."

Jonathan's eyes widened. "Did they say who it was?"

Lisa shook her head. "No, only that he might be able to help them solve this case. That's why I'm going, because my husband sometimes gets into things over his head when he thinks there may be a story involved. I've found that there's often a very fine line between bravery and stupidity."

Jonathan grunted his agreement.

Lisa said, "Do you know who this guy is they're going to see? Is it the same guy *we're* going to see?"

Jonathan took in a deep breath. "Yeah, it's probably the same guy. I might as well level with you, though, and tell you that 'this guy' is my grandfather. In fact, he's my great-grandfather ten times removed. My parents were both killed in a diving accident when I was still a toddler. Caesar took me in and cared for me like his own son. He and Blackbeard were inseparable up until Blackbeard's death. My grandfather, in fact, was the one who introduced Blackbeard and the other pirates to the one they called The Teacher, or the Death Defier. Caesar came into possession of a very old book, passed down to him from the Death Defier, that contained spells and incantations that could do amazing things, like move inanimate objects and raise the dead. But there were other secrets in this book that even

Caesar and Blackbeard would not dare to unlock, things beyond your worst nightmares."

Lisa sat in stunned silence. Eventually, she found her voice again. "You're telling me this shaman is the original Caesar Jefferson, from 1718? He's been alive and living in Charleston all these years and nobody has noticed?"

"Not exactly. He hasn't always lived in Charleston. When people he knows begin to get up in age, he moves to a different town in order to avoid detection. It looks a little weird when your friends are all ninety years old and you still don't look a day over sixty. All of his wives have died and all of his children, as well, but he hasn't bothered to remarry in years. I do have a few cousins living here and there, though most of them are twice my age."

"May I ask exactly how he has managed to stay alive all these years?"

"You may ask, but to tell you the truth, I'm not really sure. All I know is that he learned it from The Teacher. It's probably in the very book we're searching for."

They sat silently for a while, the SUV's big tires humming on the highway like giant bees in a hive.

Then Lisa asked Jonathan, "Has he ever sacrificed anyone?"

Jonathan Jefferson remained unnervingly quiet.

The cabbie eyed the odd pair standing under the streetlamp by the boat docks—the small, balding geek of a man with glasses, and the hulking biker with shaggy black hair and jet-black beard who looked as if he could snap a tree trunk in half with his bare hands.

George Forehand had been driving cabs for nearly forty years up and down the streets of Charleston. He'd driven everything from drunken sailors to abused spouses and runaway teenagers in his taxi. He had even been held up a couple of times, and thankfully had escaped with his life. But there was an overwhelming darkness, an evil presence surrounding these two that made him want to keep driving past them.

Almost.

As he got closer to them, however, his hands and feet would not obey his brain. George felt a drop of sweat creep down his bald head as some invisible force directed him to pull his Yellow Cab over to the curb. The short one opened the door, allowing the big man to get into the back seat. George watched in the rearview mirror as the cab tilted to one side, then righted itself when the smaller man got in on the other side.

"Where to?" he asked after the geek closed his door.

The big man spoke, and his low baritone, calm as the night sky, held an underlying animosity that chilled George to the bone. "Drive where I say. Understand?"

George spied the man's piercing, green eyes in the rearview mirror, and he suddenly felt as though he was sleeping. Was he dreaming this? He no longer felt like himself, but rather like a prisoner looking out through the bars of a cell as the world whizzed by.

George continued to stare into the mirror at his two strange passengers. The bead of sweat trickled down his forehead and dripped off his nose onto his pants leg.

"Sure. I understand," he said without conviction.

George pulled out from the curb and didn't even bother to start his meter, driving off into the night and thinking to himself that when he woke up he would seriously consider retiring from the taxi business.

Hunter lay on the floor in the darkness, staring up at the ceiling. He had decided to rough it and let his friend Summerfield have the couch. It was only around ten o'clock, but all of them were exhausted. They had talked for hours, Hunter asking questions about Caesar's amazing life and about the book he had written some two-hundred-and-fifty years ago. But Hunter was still dubious about his true age. Could a man really live three centuries? People had lived that long in the Bible, Hunter remembered, some for nearly a thousand years, but it was always difficult to tell which stories in the Bible were fables and which were fact.

Caesar told of amazing adventures, of how he had run away as a young slave and joined up with Blackbeard and his gang. Because he was strong and able to handle himself in a fight, they accepted him as one of them, not judging him by his station in life or the color of his skin. He had even seen women pirates, he had said. But the life of a pirate was extremely harsh, and not at all the romantic enterprise many thought it to be. The weather at sea was more often than not at odds with pirate travel plans, howling winds beating their sails like bed sheets whipping in a hurricane, driving them back a mile for every two that they gained. Then there was the hardtack and salted pork the men ate on long voyages, and the diseases that often ravaged the crew.

But the material wealth made up for the hardships.

They were usually met with animosity wherever they went, and found it difficult to gain anything other than the most shallow friendship or romance, usually in the form of a prostitute. Edward Teach had been somewhat of a ladies' man, Caesar said, becoming infatuated with even the lowest bar maid, often taking them down to the nearest magistrate to be married. It was said he had seventeen wives, but no one could remember the exact count. Blackbeard had apparently taken to heart the saying, *A girl in every port.*

Blackbeard had also been a fierce fighter, Caesar said, carrying up to eight single-shot pistols in holsters strapped to his torso, and a long cutlass, with which he was an expert swordsman. At one point, Blackbeard had traveled to the Orient and had become adept in what was now called martial arts. Teach could fight barehanded better than any man he had ever seen, his hands deft and quick as lightning. The stories about Teach wearing lit fuses in his hair, using the smoke to create the illusion of a fiery demon, was also true. Caesar told them that Blackbeard—as big and as tall as Caesar—was already a frightful enough sight to behold without such enhancements.

As a friend, however, Caesar was adamant that Blackbeard was as loyal as they came, willing to lay down his life, if necessary. In the heat of battle, Blackbeard had more than once taken a bullet in the arm or the leg so that one of his crewmen would avoid harm. When they were sick or wounded, he tended to them like a caring physician would, bringing them food and medicine. His officers and men were disciplined and showed him great reverence, impressing the captains and crews of many a ship. He even loved children, handing out gold pieces and candy whenever he would meet them in port.

Of course, like most people, Blackbeard had a dark side, albeit a little darker than most. Once, while in drunken revelry, Blackbeard had been playing cards with some of the crew when he suddenly pulled out his pistol and shot his first mate, Israel Hands, in the knee underneath the table, crippling him for life. The unfortunate Hands immediately slid out of his seat onto the floor, wailing in pain, before being taken to sick bay.

"Just so nobody forgets who I am," Blackbeard had

said.

Blackbeard was a walking paradox, Hunter thought.

In his mind, Hunter imagined the pirate guzzling rum and saying, "Yo, ho ho." Those images began to mingle with things Caesar had told them, becoming more like a confused fairy tale. Hunter smiled at this. Slowly, the images began to fade as he slipped off into sleep, his eyelids growing heavy.

His fuzzy brain barely registered the sound of the front door creaking open, and the long, dark shadow that spilled across the living room floor.

As Jonathan stepped into his great-grandfather's darkened house, he motioned for Lisa to come inside, then quietly turned to close the door. That was when he noticed movement out of the corner of his eye.

"Lisa?" he heard someone say, and turned to see a dark-haired man moving towards them. Jonathan made the mistake of grabbing the man by the wrist.

The man immediately stepped back, lowering his arm and pulling Jonathan off balance. As Jonathan straightened and tried to regain balance, the guy delivered a lightning quick blow to Jonathan's face, sending him sprawling across the floor.

"Hunter, no!" Lisa shouted too late.

The lights suddenly flicked on, momentarily blinding them all. Jonathan, seeing stars, looked up at his opponent and rubbed his aching jaw. He noticed that there was also another man, tall and blond, standing by the couch, looking half asleep and watching the proceedings with mild amusement.

"Ow," Jonathan said. "I should have known better than that. Don't tell me, Kung Fu, right? I recognize the move."

Hunter looked perplexed, standing sideways to his opponent, expecting him to jump up and attack. "Who the hell are you?" he asked.

"Hunter, this is Jonathan Jefferson," Lisa said. "Jonathan *Caesar* Jefferson, great-grandson of Caesar."

At that same instant, a door opened and Caesar himself bounded into the room, pulling up the zipper on a faded pair of blue jeans. He observed the scene before him, then let out a mild chuckle. "I see everyone has met my great-grandson, overzealous as always, sticking his nose where it doesn't belong."

Jonathan picked himself up off the floor, dusting off the seat of his pants. He extended a hand to Hunter. "Jonathan Jefferson. Glad to meet you."

Hunter looked at the extended hand, then at Jonathan. After an awkward silence, he shook the man's hand. "Hunter Singleton."

Lisa had to fight to keep from smiling. "I hope you two are done beating the crap out of each other."

"Us two?" Jonathan said, rubbing his jaw for effect. "Hubby here is the one doing all the beating."

"I guess I don't have to ask if you got my message. I can see you did," Hunter said, dropping his fight stance and eyeing Lisa.

"Yes, I did. And I think you're crazy for taking the law into your own hands. You don't know what you're up against, Hunter. This is for the law to handle."

Everyone in the room focused on the pair, watching one then the other like a crowd rotating their heads at a tennis match.

"Ha! The law? You mean you?" Hunter turned his back and walked to the other side of the room, then turned to face Lisa. "This guy Blackbeard or whoever he is, is a maniac. I believe he has some kind of supernatural power and no law in the world is going to stop him."

"I realize that. That's why Jonathan and I are here."

Hunter glanced at Jonathan suspiciously. "What is he, your new boyfriend?"

Lisa walked a straight line to Hunter, grabbed his face in both hands, and gave him a kiss that electrified him down to his toes.

Hunter stood staring at Lisa, a look of slack-jawed confusion on his face. Jonathan and Caesar snickered, as Jason Summerfield let out a good-natured "woo!"

Lisa said, "I tried to call you, Hunter, to tell you not to come to Charleston, and to tell you how I feel about you.

But junior over here," she jerked a thumb back over her shoulder at Jonathan, "interrupted me."

Jonathan glanced over at his grandfather with a hurt look on his face, pointing at himself and mouthing the word, "*junior?*"

Hunter looked over at Jonathan, still not quite comprehending the whole thing.

"Hunter," Lisa said, regaining his attention, "I just wanted to tell you that I still love you. I want to start over again, if you'll have me."

Hunter was completely thunderstruck. Lisa's words sounded like a melodic song to him. He never imagined in his wildest dreams that Lisa would come back to him, after all he had put her through. "Of *course* I'll take you back," he said.

Hunter barely got the words out when the front door crashed open against the wall and a hulking figure with flowing black hair and a wide, yellow-toothed grin filled the doorframe.

Hunter couldn't believe what he was seeing. The man standing in the doorway was huge, bigger than he had imagined. He didn't seem to be carrying any weapons, which relieved him somewhat. The man wore khaki pants, a white button down shirt and black shoes, but in spite of the modern, casual dress, Teach was still an intimidating presence. His skin was white, but wind and sun had scorched it red. He looked to be no more than thirty years old, let alone three-hundred. The group stood, eyeing one another, waiting for someone to make the first move.

Caesar finally spoke in his African-accented English. "It didn't take long for you to find me."

The group looked from Caesar to Teach, wondering if the pirate would speak.

Teach narrowed his eyes at Caesar and spoke slowly, deliberately, recounting the time since Blackbeard's death like a man remembering torture at the hands of his enemy. But Hunter knew it was the demon, the Diablero, that spoke and not Teach himself.

"For almost three-hundred years I have been trapped inside the bones of this . . . mortal. The sea is like a tomb, cold and dark, the sand shifting with the tides, burying me alive slowly, inch by painful inch. If I were human I would have been driven mad. But I have been freed from the chains that bind me, and now I have come for you."

To Hunter, the words flowed from the demon's mouth almost like some macabre poetry.

They all turned to face Caesar, who stared directly at Blackbeard with an unflinching gaze.

"I am ready. But know that I do not go willingly and I

will fight you if I have the chance."

Blackbeard grinned a deadly, lopsided grin.

"You won't have the chance," he replied.

John Aiden stepped through the open doorway with his Glock drawn and pointed straight at Caesar. A ripple of surprise went through the room at the man's sudden appearance.

Instinctively, Lisa drew the pistol from her shoulder holster. She crouched and held the gun steady with both hands, ready to fire, ready to blow away the intruder if need be. "Drop your weapon, sir!" she yelled, "or I'll be forced to shoot."

Teach turned on Lisa, as if seeing her for the first time, and waved a hand at Aiden to lower his gun. Aiden lowered the Glock reluctantly.

"Well, what do we have here?" Teach whispered, slowly moving toward Lisa.

Lisa decided to shift her aim from Aiden to Teach. "Stop right there, big guy, or I'll shoot you where it counts."

Just then, Lisa's gun started moving, writhing in her hand like a steel snake trying to escape her grip. She let out a yelp and dropped the gun to the floor. She made a move to try to pick it up, but when she did, the pistol began writhing again, the barrel and the butt of the gun moving up and down as if they were alive and angry. The group stared, dumbfounded at the pistol as it bounced around on the floor.

The demon smiled and glanced down at the gun. "I don't think your weapon is going to cooperate."

The gun twisted itself butt to barrel, forming a half-circle, then lay still on the floor.

Teach looked up at Lisa, and Hunter thought he could see fire in the demon's eyes.

"I would like you to accompany me on my journey. I'm sure your presence would make the trip most enjoyable."

Hunter felt an angry heat burning in his chest. He

stepped in front of Lisa and held up a hand toward Blackbeard. "Oh no you don't, Captain Hook. You'll have to go through me first."

Hunter saw the look in Teach's eyes go from lust to fury in a split second. "Who the fuck are you?" Teach bellowed, but the sound was like several voices speaking in unison. Hunter knew he was hearing the multi-voiced utterances of a demon.

But Hunter's pride would never allow him to back down from a fight, even with a demon. "*I'm* her *man*, motherfucker! I'm her fucking husband, that's who I am!" he bellowed back.

Lisa was frantic. "Hunter please. This is no ordinary man. He can do things to you . . ."

Hunter didn't let her finish. He took two quick steps and let loose with a flying kick to Blackbeard's face.

But the pirate moved amazingly fast, faster than Hunter thought possible, and he grabbed Hunter by the heel and gave it a yank, putting him down hard on his back. Hunter had the wind knocked out of him and lay on the floor, gasping for breath.

Blackbeard didn't hide his contempt for him and his efforts at protecting his wife. "Is that the best you can do, little man?"

Hunter finally caught his breath and looked up at the demon, then suddenly felt a charge of adrenaline course through his body. "No, it's not," he hissed, jumping up off the floor with one fluid movement. He stood in a fighting stance, ready for Blackbeard to come at him.

Instead, Hunter himself began to move, but not under his own power. His feet slid across the floor toward Blackbeard as if they were being pulled by an invisible rope. Hunter was helpless to stop it. He looked down at his feet, then back up at the pirate, who was getting closer by the second.

No one in the room knew what to do, all watching as the inevitable played out.

Teach held out a meaty hand and wrapped it around Hunter's throat, then lifted him straight up off the floor. Hunter's feet dangled like a man hanging from a noose. Stars began to fill his vision as he struggled for air. He grabbed at the pirate's arm, but it was as solid and unyielding as a flesh-covered steel pipe.

Lisa finally found her voice and ran toward the pair, screaming her plea at Teach. "Stop it! You're killing him!"

Teach looked down at Lisa as if she were a child being punished for bad behavior. "What do you offer in return?"

Lisa knew she had no choice. Hunter was beginning to lose consciousness and she knew he would soon be dead if she did not act quickly. "I'll go with you. But promise me you'll let him live."

"I promise *nothing*," Teach growled.

Hunter could hear Teach's voice, then Lisa's voice, but the words faded in and out like a dream. Was it a dream? He didn't know, he only knew that he desperately needed to draw a breath.

Just one heavenly breath was all he asked.

But instead, darkness slowly began to envelop him like a warm blanket, and he welcomed it with open arms.

Part II
The Great Old Ones

… And I saw a star fall from heaven unto the Earth, and to him was given the key of the bottomless pit. And he opened the bottomless pit …

Revelation 9: 1-2

Before me things create were none, save things Eternal, and eternal I endure.
All hope abandon, ye who enter here.

Dante's Inferno

Lisa sat in the back of Caesar's huge Buick, wedged between the creepy little man and Jonathan, whom Teach had insisted come along. Lisa was actually glad he had come. Caesar drove the car while Teach sat up front, and Aiden's Glock kept the odds even. Of course, no one wanted to go up against a man with supernatural powers, so Lisa thought the Glock to be unnecessary under the circumstances. Aiden's leg kept inadvertently rubbing up against hers. She shuddered at his touch and tried scooting closer to Jonathan, hoping she wasn't sending the wrong message.

She thought of Hunter and hoped he was all right. She had checked his pulse after Teach dropped him on the floor. Weak but steady. She wished he had come with them; for some reason, he and Summerfield had been spared. She just prayed he didn't try to follow them. But Lisa just knew Hunter would try. He would follow them to Hell and back if need be.

Lisa eyed Caesar in the front seat and knew from his set jaw and steely gaze that he was conflicted. The man wanted to stop Blackbeard, but knew he would be jeopardizing his grandson's life and possibly hers if he wasn't compliant. Lisa wondered what kind of power Caesar could possess that was greater than that of a demon, so much so that the demon would raise a body from the dead and walk the Earth to find him. What was Teach after? What kind of force could be so powerful? What could be in this book of his that was so important that death itself could not even keep Teach from it? Lisa thought back to her dream and the demonic eyes that stared up from under the water, the skeletal hand that reached up and pulled her into the blackness. On other nights, voices—dark and disembodied—spoke to her of profane and monstrous things that she dared not remember when she woke up, for fear that she may never sleep again.

As Lisa thought of these things, Blackbeard craned his neck and looked at her, a nearly imperceptible smile playing on his lips. Her stomach turned to a knot with the look and she had to avert her eyes, training them on Caesar once again.

Lisa had had enough of the silence. "Caesar, can you tell me where we're going?"

Caesar looked over at Teach, who said nothing, but turned to stare out the windshield once again.

"If I had to guess, I'd say San Salvador."

Lisa scrunched her brow. "San Salvador?"

Jonathan nodded. "I believe it's called Cat Island now. Part of the outer islands of the Bahamas. Lots of caves there. A good place to hide treasure and . . . other things."

Caesar glanced at Blackbeard, who remained stoic.

Suddenly, Lisa got an idea. She casually slipped her right hand into her pocket and found the cell phone, then clicked it on and, with her thumb, slowly began punching in numbers on the keypad.

Hunter woke up on the floor of Caesar's house, wondering where the freight train was that had hit him. As his eyes adjusted to the light, his friend Jason Summerfield began to come into focus.

"What . . . what the hell happened?" he rasped as he tried to sit up.

Summerfield gently pushed him back down and onto the pillow. "Don't try to get up yet. You need to rest for a moment. You're lucky you weren't killed."

Hunter was struck with a sudden realization. "Lisa. We have got to save Lisa," he said, trying to sit up.

Summerfield pushed him back down.

Hunter looked around, noticed he and Summerfield were the only two in the room. "Where are they?"

Summerfield sighed in resignation. "Gone. Blackbeard took Lisa, and Jonathan and Caesar went with them. I think Blackbeard said he had a boat somewhere, waiting to pick them up."

"Pick them up?" Hunter managed to sit up straight, his head swimming with the effort. He grimaced at the sudden pain. "And take them where? Do you know where they were going?" Hunter was almost ready to grab Summerfield by the shoulders and shake him.

"I think so. I think they're going to an island, a place in the Bahamas called Providence. It was a port frequented by Blackbeard during his lifetime. If the accounts I've read are true, I believe that what he's looking for may be there."

"How can we be sure? Is there a way to follow them?"

Summerfield grinned. "Funny you should ask. It just so happens I know of a place where we can get a boat. Or, I should say, a yacht. A forty-footer, very well-equipped for the high seas."

Hunter shook his head in wonder. "Why am I not surprised?" He held out a hand, and Summerfield stood and gave Hunter a lift up off the floor. Hunter's head reeled, and he steadied himself like a man trying to get his sea legs.

"Remind me not to pick fights with guys who can lift you from the floor with one hand."

Summerfield chuckled. "Yeah, you looked kind of like a rag doll hanging there. He could have crushed your throat if he wanted to, you know. Or worse."

Hunter rubbed his neck, wincing at the raw tenderness there. "Yeah. He could have crushed my soul, right? How long was I out, anyway?"

"I don't know; ten minutes, maybe less. I thought you were dead when you hit the floor."

Hunter looked around the room once more, and realized there was something gleaming on the floor in front of the living room door. He walked over and picked it up, recognition sweeping across his face. It was a small silver cross encrusted with diamonds.

"Lisa's necklace. I gave this to her on our very first wedding anniversary. But how did it fall off?"

Summerfield looked at Hunter as if he didn't know how to frame the words. "It didn't fall off, exactly. Blackbeard saw it and ripped it off of her just before they left."

Hunter stiffened, then closed his fist tightly around the pendant. "Why would he do that?"

"Why do you think? He's a demon. Demons abhor anything that reminds them of who they are, of *what* they are. The old battle of good versus evil."

Hunter's heart ached for Lisa and he couldn't stand the thought of her with that . . . *thing*. His veins burned with fire as he tried to focus his mind on a solution, a way to get his wife back. Nothing else mattered.

"We have to find them," he said. "I don't care what it takes or what it costs, we have to find them. Where is this boat you were talking about? Is it close?"

"It's in the harbor, fueled-up and ready to go."

"We have to leave as soon as possible. Do we need to get anyone to pilot the boat?"

Summerfield took a small bow. "I'm ready when you are, my captain."

The night in Charleston harbor was black and moonless. The further away from the city they traveled, the smaller Aiden's sixty-foot yacht seemed to Lisa. The darkness was like an endless void, swallowing them whole. The twin engines hummed as the knife-edge of the bow cut a path through the inky water. The lights of passing boats dotted the landscape like fireflies.

Lisa was glad she had decided to wear jeans. It was chilly on the water, and the pants also hid her legs. Though Blackbeard had not made a move to touch her or even speak to her, she did not want to be ogled by him or Jonathan, or that other weird little guy driving the boat, John Aiden, who seemed to be along just for the ride.

Lisa couldn't believe all the things that had happened the last few hours. If she had not been the one living it and someone else had told her the story, she would have said they were nuts. But here she was, on a boat with a demon, a psycho, a shaman, and his grandson. What a motley crew, she thought. She regretted the fact that there had been so little time to work out things with Hunter. She hoped there would be more time in the future. But things at the moment were looking bleak. What did they hope to accomplish by finding this book? Was it really as powerful as Jonathan made it out to be? If the lure was enough to bring back a man from the dead, then Lisa guessed the stories about the book probably were true.

And that scared her.

She looked around the boat from her place at the stern. Blackbeard stood motionless on the bow, his black hair and beard tossed in the wind, gazing as if he could see what lay ahead in the darkness. Perhaps he could, Lisa thought. With the powers of a demon, he could most likely see things the rest of them only had nightmares about. She wondered what he was thinking, what he was really after, his ultimate goal. Then again, maybe she was better off not knowing.

Suddenly, he looked at her. She stood still as a statue, transfixed by his gaze. Was he putting her under some kind of spell? Was this the same thing women had felt when Blackbeard once had a female in every port? His intense, hazel eyes made her feel naked, like there was nothing she could hide, nowhere she could run to escape his scrutiny. Yet, somehow, his eyes also spoke to her, told her things she didn't want to hear, called her name, whispering . . . *Lisa, Lisa . . .*

A sudden touch on her arm startled her. She looked up to see Jonathan smiling down at her, then turned back to see that Blackbeard was no longer looking at her. Had the whole thing been her imagination?

"Hey, you should go down below and check out the amenities," Jonathan said. "Aiden said you could have the big stateroom with the queen-sized bed."

Lisa rolled her eyes. "I'm flattered."

"There's even a shower and a kitchen. Come on, I'll show you around."

Jonathan opened the door to the lower deck, and he and Lisa disappeared inside.

Liang Wu tried his daughter's cell phone again, and once again his gut instinct, honed from his years in law enforcement, told him something was wrong. The text message she had sent him only hours after her phone call left him with a feeling of apprehension. It had said only two words—Cat Island.

Was that where she was heading? And why send him a text and not call him? It wasn't like her, unless she was trying to hide the message from someone. That had to be it. And if that was true, that meant she was likely under some sort of duress.

As he pulled up close to Lisa's apartment, he saw the complex in his headlights. Liang steered his Jeep Cherokee into a parking space a few spaces down from Lisa's apartment and turned off the engine. He reached into his glove compartment and pulled out his .44 Magnum, checked the chambers, and stepped out of the car. He closed the door quietly, then bumped it shut with his hip so as not to make noise.

Liang stuck the gun into his waistband and carefully walked toward the apartment. From where he was, he could see there were no lights inside, which could mean Lisa either left before dark or was still inside and somehow disabled.

Or, God forbid, dead.

He made his way up the steps and peered through the door window. There didn't seem to be anyone inside and the furniture was still in place. No broken lamps or overturned chairs. He pulled out his key and let himself in.

Once inside, Liang made his way to every room in the house, every closet and the utility room. His daughter was nowhere to be found.

On the bar sat a glass of half-finished tea. Liang remembered the message she had left earlier in the day, telling him about Jonathan and the message from Hunter. If only he had picked up the phone instead of sleeping like the old man he was becoming. He could have kicked himself.

He looked over at Lisa's phone, then walked to it and pressed the Play button on the answering machine. The last few messages played, some from him, others from friends, but the one from Hunter was the one that he found the most interesting. Liang stood, listening with intense interest, trying to put together what he was hearing with what Lisa had told him on the phone and the text message she had sent. It didn't quite add up, but he knew something had to be done. As an ex-cop, he knew the consequences of waiting until it was too late. Time to be proactive.

The message finished playing through twice, and Liang picked up the phone and punched in the number of an old friend. After a few rings, a familiar voice sounded on the other end, and Liang felt a wave of relief. He did his best to keep his voice as calm as possible.

"Jimmy, I think we have a problem."

Teach had been taught in the Royal Navy that women and ships did not belong together, that women were bad luck. As a pirate, however, he had seen more than one woman bring a man to his knees with a cutlass or a well-aimed pistol shot. Female pirates were rare, but he had found them to be as formidable as their male counterparts.

Lisa could easily be one of these women. As beautiful as any he had ever seen, with her mix of Asian and African features, she was also lethal and would make either a loyal friend or a deadly enemy. He decided that to take her by force would be unwise. To truly have her loyalty, he would have to allow her to come to him of her own free will. He was doubtful of whether this would happen, since she seemed to have feelings for this Hunter. But Blackbeard had always had a way with women. He'd never met one he couldn't eventually seduce, whether she was married or not.

As for Jonathan and Caesar, they would become part of his crew. He knew they had no loyalty towards him, but it wouldn't matter once they were dead. Then, he would raise them and they would be his followers. He would have a crew such as the world had never seen; an army of the dead. They would walk the Earth, enforcing his will, and he would reign supreme. The spell from the book would make him invincible, forever tying him to this world, giving him powers beyond anything these mortals could ever imagine. Even now, his power was great enough to withstand any force the humans could throw at him.

It was laughable to think that one of them had been stupid enough to bring him back from the dead, to evoke the spell of reincarnation, but he had. For now, that person still held sway over his spirit, but not for long. Soon, that would change, and the man would pay with his life.

He reveled in the senses of this body, this new, yet old, body that had been rebuilt cell-upon-cell from virtually nothing. Even he, as a demon, did not fully understand how it worked, but knew he had been allowed to do many things not usually given to those of his kind. Their place had been reserved in the pit, in the darkness, behind the veil where light and love and goodness are merely concepts, things that exist in principle. For him and his brethren, they did not exist at all. Only hate and fear and pain were realities in their world.

But here, in this mortal body, he experienced things that had, at first, frightened him, because they were beyond his understanding, beyond his experience. He knew that at one time, they had lived in the light, had known peace and joy, but that had been many forgotten eons ago. This thing he was feeling for the woman was something he had no inkling of, because it didn't come from him. It came from the other, from Edward Teach, the one who was supposed to have been killed.

But the demon knew he was more powerful than the man, and he would keep it under his power, as he had when he first wrested control of this body from its original owner.

Teach looked up at the night sky and recognized every constellation, every star, every planet. He knew exactly where they were and exactly how far they had to go. But he had no desire to sleep. He found he didn't need more than four hours a night, sometimes less. And eating or drinking was almost nonexistent, being more of a pleasure than an outright necessity. He thought he might at some point go to the boat's galley and try to see what type of food was aboard. Whatever it was, he was sure it would be much better than the salted pork and hardtack that passed for a sailor's sustenance in his day.

He turned to look at the pilothouse and saw that Aiden was gone and Caesar had taken over the wheel.

Lisa lay fully dressed in the darkness, the hum of the boat's twin diesels a little louder than she would have liked. But then again, *none* of this was to her liking. The boat bobbed and rocked in the waves. The surf seemed to grow choppier as they sailed south to the Bahamas. At first, she felt a little seasick, but the feeling soon passed. She was too exhausted to let it affect her. Lisa had been out on boats many times in the Albemarle Sound as a ranger, and was an ardent kayaker, as well. She knew the water, had grown up around it.

The boat's shower had felt good on her skin, the warm water washing away the grime, cleansing away the dirtiness she felt. Was she a traitor, or a hero? She wasn't sure. She only hoped she was doing the right thing, that events were happening the way they were supposed to. She had to have faith that they were.

Lisa was glad she had brought along a change of clothes. It would have been nice to have her gun, as well, but after the demon had twisted it into a pretzel, it was useless, anyway. Besides, how could you kill something that was already dead?

She thought about the events at Caesar's house and wondered what had happened to Hunter. Jason Summerfield swore to her that he would look after Hunter, and she knew he would. Seeing them both together was always a little strange; two of her ex-lovers.

After the ordeal at Caesar's, the ride in his car felt as if she was riding to her death. She had never been so afraid. Once they got to the boat, she wondered what Blackbeard, or any of the others, would do to her.

So far, it seemed, her fears had been unfounded, though

she had caught Aiden eyeing her on more than one occasion. He was a seedy little man, looking at everyone and everything with suspicion in his eyes. She wondered what his game was.

She listened to the waves lapping the side of the boat outside her open portal, the wind gently blowing her hair. The moonlight cast a faint glow upon the bed, and she wished Hunter was there beside her, telling her everything would be all right, that there was nothing to fear, no dead pirates walking around, no demons, no secret books, just the two of them.

She smiled for the first time in days, then glanced at the stateroom door.

The brass doorknob began to turn slowly.

Hunter eyed the beat-up old Buick sitting by the docks and had a sudden sinking feeling in the pit of his stomach. Although he knew how brave Lisa was, he also realized she was probably terrified, wondering to herself if she would live to see another day. He swore that if Blackbeard or Jonathan so much as touched her, he would rip out their beating hearts and shove them down their throats. He was pretty sure Caesar was trustworthy, but he knew that sometimes a person you trusted most could turn out to be your worst enemy.

He glanced at Summerfield. "I hope you're right about where they're headed. What if we get there and find out you were wrong? Then what?"

"Don't worry." Summerfield smiled. "I'm not wrong. And besides, I have a foolproof means of tracking them to their destination, whatever it might be."

Summerfield reached into his pocket and pulled out a small, black box with a large LCD, several buttons, and the words *MAGELLAN* written in big block letters.

Hunter recognized the device immediately. "A GPS system," he said, a knowing smile crossing his lips.

"Yep. We can track their location, speed, and direction."

"Where is the transmitter?"

"In the best place I could think of to put it—Caesar's pocket."

Hunter slowly nodded his head. "Good move. As long as Blackbeard doesn't decide to throw him overboard, that is."

"Don't worry, that won't happen. Blackbeard needs Caesar to decipher the book for him and to cast the proper spell. Otherwise, it's just meaningless words."

Hunter walked beside Summerfield as they moved toward the pier. "What kind of boat did you say you had? Is it a rental?"

"No, it belonged to my father. When he passed away, he left it to me, along with the payments. Luckily, it was mostly paid off."

"I never knew you had a boat. Why do you keep it here? Why not bring it to River City, put it in the marina?"

"Since Dad lived in Myrtle Beach, he liked to keep it parked in Charleston to avoid the tourist traffic, as if there's no tourist traffic here. I just never got around to moving it, I guess. Too much trouble. And besides, I spend a lot of time down here. Reminds me of my childhood."

They came to a boardwalk lined with long wooden piers, each berth occupied with everything from small fishing boats and trawlers to yachts and twin-hulled catamarans. Since it was night, the boardwalk was mostly deserted. Dim lights shone from the windows on some of the boats, providing subtle signs of occupancy. A true boat-lover's paradise. Hunter shook his head in amazement.

"So, which one's ours?" he asked.

Summerfield turned down one of the piers. Hunter followed close behind, then stopped in front of the sleekest, most aerodynamic boat he had ever seen. They walked down a short gangplank to the main deck. Being ex-Navy, Hunter was familiar with most types of boats. He could see this one had an eighteen-to-twenty-foot beam and was about forty feet long from stem to stern. The pilothouse sat atop a bridge surrounded by dark, Plexiglas windows and a lower deck that likely held a berthing area and probably a kitchen and a head. The bow swept to a perfect knife-edge, topped by a stainless steel railing that encircled the boat. On the stern, a ladder led down to a deck for diving.

On the starboard side, near the water line, was a name, which was a little too dark to make out.

Summerfield suddenly appeared from the pilothouse

and looked down at Hunter. "Welcome aboard the *Gertrude*, named after my mother," he said.

Hunter was awestruck. "Nice boat," he said, nodding approvingly.

Then he flung his backpack over his shoulder and walked across the gangplank.

Lisa stared at the brass door handle of her stateroom.

She lay as still as the dead, holding her breath until she thought she might turn blue. She had the same feeling she did when she was a little girl living in the country in northeastern North Carolina and a particularly nasty nor'easter had come up. The near-hurricane-force winds howled relentlessly, the branches from a nearby willow tree slapping out a rhythm against the side of her house like a ghost beating out Morse code, signaling it was time to die. But as she watched the door swing wide and the dim light pour inside, she knew this was much more real than a little girl's frightened imagination.

She couldn't tell if it was relief or just a lower level of fear when she realized it was John Aiden—and not the Death Defier—standing in the doorway. He looked at her and smiled, and the smile reminded her of something she had once seen on the face of a wanted sex-offender.

"Sorry to bother you, but I was in the galley and wondered if maybe you might want something to eat. I have plenty of food and plenty to drink. Even some wine. Good stuff from a local Williamsburg winery."

Lisa could feel her heart racing. She wondered who was piloting the boat. Somehow she managed to keep her voice calm. "No, thanks. I was just about to go to sleep, actually."

"That's why I didn't knock. I was afraid I might wake you. But since you weren't asleep, I thought I'd offer some food. While I'm here, though, let me just show you how the ventilation system works in this room, in case you get cold."

Quicker than she could react, Aiden was in her room,

the door closed behind him. He flicked on the light and began fiddling with a device on her wall that looked somewhat like a thermostat. She sat up in the bed and watched with rising alarm.

"It looks like it's set. I think you should be pretty comfortable," Aiden said, his back turned to her.

"Thanks, but the window's open anyway and I really would like to go to sleep now, if you don't—"

When Aiden turned, Lisa saw him clutching a large butcher knife in his hand. She couldn't imagine where he had concealed it. Instinctively, she jumped against the backboard of her bed.

"If you so much as make a sound, I'll cut your goddamned head off!" he hissed.

"I knew there was something wrong with you. What do you want, you freak?"

"What any red-blooded male would want, of course. I've been watching you, prancing around in those tight jeans all night long. I can tell you have a great body, that you work out. I'll bet you break a lot of hearts with that face, too, and those lips . . ." he trailed off, and a bead of sweat trickled down the side of his face.

"Listen, we can talk about this, just—"

"Shut up, or I *will* rape you! Luckily for you, I'm in a hurry, so I'll make it easy for you."

Aiden clamped the knife blade between his teeth like a B-movie Tarzan, and watching Lisa intently, he reached down and unbuckled his pants, letting them fall to his knees. She saw with disgust that he wasn't wearing underwear, and already had an erection. He grabbed the knife in his hand and pointed the blade at her. "Now let's see what you can do with that mouth besides talk."

Lisa wasn't sure what happened next, but somehow Teach appeared in her room, standing over Aiden like a mountain towering over a lone pine tree. The door to her stateroom remained closed.

Lisa watched as the look on Aiden's face changed from

lust to fear as he sensed Blackbeard's presence behind him. The knife fell from his hand and clattered uselessly on the teakwood deck as he slowly turned to face the demon.

"I . . . I was just having a little fun, that's all. I wasn't going to hurt her, I swear."

Lisa could see two large hands grab Aiden by the shoulders, and the little man, his bare ass hanging out, was lifted up off the deck by almost a foot. But the hands weren't hands at all; they were more like the claws of a bird, like those of a monstrous eagle. When the Death Defier spoke, his voice boomed so loudly Lisa thought the walls of the small stateroom might explode. Listening to it, she felt as if she might go insane, and put her hands over her ears.

"Leave the wench alone, Aiden. And if I catch you again, I'll flay you alive and send you straight to Hell, where you belong. Understood?"

Aiden, grasping for the second time at the steel-muscled arms that held him, forced a feeble "yes" through his dry larynx before Teach released his grip and Aiden came crashing to the deck.

"Now get out."

Aiden got up off the deck as quickly as he could, stumbling and pulling up his pants as he tried to open the stateroom door.

When he got it open, Jonathan stood outside. "Is everything okay?" he asked. "I heard a crash and some yelling and thought somebody might be in trouble."

Aiden quickly shot past him, and Jonathan watched him go, then turned and went into the stateroom.

On the bed, Lisa sat, staring at an empty wall.

Blackbeard was gone.

H unter and Summerfield sat in the pilothouse of the forty-two-foot Regal Express yacht, which Hunter still couldn't believe belonged to his friend. He knew the family had money. Summerfield's father had been a prominent physician in Myrtle Beach before he had contracted cancer and had to quit his practice. But still, the yacht had to be worth nearly a half-million, easy. Must be nice to be rich, he thought.

The only boat Hunter's family had ever owned was the one he and his father took to Lake Tenkiller in Muskogee, Oklahoma, when they went fishing. It had a small, single outboard Evinrude engine that coughed and sputtered when they tried to start it, but it got the job done. They usually managed to come back with a bass or two and an empty drink cooler.

Hunter looked down over the side of the boat. They sliced through the water at about thirty knots. He could see the electrolytes glowing green as the hull generated friction in the salty sea.

Hunter looked up at the stars and remembered his time in the Navy, staring up at the same sky and feeling as small as a grain of sand on an endless beach. He was always amazed at the sheer number of stars that were visible once out and away from civilization and city lights. Sometimes, between standing watches in the engine room and sleeping, he would climb up to the top of the bridge and look out through the high-powered binoculars mounted there on a swivel stand. Through them he could see the craters on the moon, Mars, Saturn, and even the moons around Jupiter. He felt like he could almost reach out and touch them.

The twin Volvo engines hummed, nearly putting him to

sleep. But Hunter knew it would be impossible to doze. He had too much on his mind. His thoughts once again turned to Lisa, where they seemed to stay most of the time. He tried his best to avoid thinking about the bizarre nature of all that had transpired in the past few days. If he thought about it too much, it made him crazy. And it made him worry about Lisa even more. He had to maintain rationality if he was to be of any help to her.

He wondered how he would ever be able to make a story out of all this, what he would tell his editor. That they had been chasing after a demon? Hunter could see no way to frame the story so that it would be believable, let alone make sense. He decided that maybe it would be best not to dwell too much on it for the time being. If and when he found Lisa and stopped Blackbeard from doing whatever it was he was determined to do with that book, he would sort it all out somehow. In the meantime, all he could do was wait, and try to enjoy the ride.

Hunter glanced over at Summerfield, who was steering the boat with a faraway look in his eyes. He wondered if Summerfield had ever taken Lisa on this yacht. He doubted it, though. The boat was obviously new, probably purchased just before Jason's father had died. Still, he was curious.

"Did you ever take Lisa out on this boat, you know, back in the day?"

Summerfield looked as if he had just snapped out of a coma and glanced over at Hunter, blinking his eyes.

"Back in the day? You mean when we were dating?" He looked perplexed by the question, then shrugged his shoulders. "Not really. We didn't own a boat then. What brought this on?" A smile crossed Summerfield's lips.

Hunter tried to look nonchalant, and gave his own shrug. "Oh, no reason, just wondering. How far would you say we can go before we have to refuel?" he asked.

"We'll stop to refuel in Miami, then go on from there. It will probably be another fifteen hours before we stop. You might want to take advantage of the time to get some sleep. You can take the main stateroom if you want. There's some food in the galley, as well, if you're hungry."

Though Hunter was grateful for the offer, he was too wound up to either eat or sleep. All he could think about was Lisa. Still, it would be nice to lay down for a while, just to try and relax, if nothing else. "I guess you talked me into it," he told Summerfield. "I'll take over for you in a few hours, just come and get me up. I want a chance to drive this baby, too, you know."

They both laughed, and Hunter got up and went down to the stateroom. In less than an hour, he was asleep.

He dreamed of Lisa, pirate ships, and vile, red-eyed demons.

He was back in her stateroom.

The lights were out, and the huge figure of Edward Teach stood like a monolith over Lisa's bed. She was a confident woman, prided herself on her fearlessness, but this was something else altogether. This was supernatural, otherworldly, and she couldn't understand how he could just appear and disappear at will. She found it unnerving, and it filled her with fear.

And yet, he had rescued her, protected her when she was about to be molested by that pervert, Aiden. Something about the pirate, a complexity of character that pointed to something deeper, something mysterious that was more than just pure evil. Somewhere in there was a man, Edward Teach.

Then he spoke to her. "Why do you fear me?"

Lisa shuddered under the blanket like an insecure child. "Because I don't understand you," she said.

"Didn't I help you in your time of need? You don't have to be afraid. I won't harm you."

"Then what do you want from me? Why are you here?"

Blackbeard turned and walked slowly to the starboard portal. He gazed out at the darkness, considering her question. Then he turned to look at her. "I'm here because I want to be here."

At least he was direct, Lisa thought.

"Why do you want to be here?" she asked.

"I wanted to look at you. You're very beautiful. John Aiden is a fool. He takes by force what should be won through seduction."

Lisa thought she saw a sly smile cross Teach's lips. She decided it might be a good time to change the subject, and she had many questions for the pirate. "Why did you kill those people in the swamp and on the island? Did they threaten you, or did they just get in the way?"

Once again Teach turned and stared through the open portal at the passing sea. "We needed them, their . . . *essence* . . . to sustain our life until we could grow a new body."

Lisa noticed the reference had changed from "I" to "we," and made a mental note of it.

"What do you mean, their essence? Do you mean their souls?"

Teach turned his eyes toward her. "If you wish."

"What do you do with their souls?"

"They stay here with us, seeing through our eyes, becoming part of us. We learn from them, gain understanding of the world around us."

Lisa was horrified to think that inside the body of Blackbeard, the souls of all those he had killed were held captive like prisoners in a dungeon. It must be hell. She imagined them, watching as if looking through a window, as the demon-possessed Teach went on his blood-drenched rampage, helpless to stop it. She wondered how many were in there.

Then, a thought occurred to her.

"Are you, Blackbeard, Edward Teach, also a prisoner?"

Teach took a step towards her, and a flash of rage darkened his face.

"We have an agreement, and the agreement stands," he bellowed. Lisa did not flinch. "We are powerful, and shall become more powerful still, and in time, you will learn to love me."

Once more, the reference had changed from "we" to "me," this time in the same sentence.

"I'm a married woman. I already have a man to love. His name is Hunter. You almost killed him."

The pirate's face softened, and a subtle look of confusion seemed to creep in momentarily.

"He . . . tried to attack me. I defended myself."

Lisa was gaining more confidence in her ability to reason with Teach, to get through to the man inside. She moved closer to the edge of the bed, looking the pirate in the eyes, which were glowing a faint red. She thought that they resembled the eyes of some feral dogs she had seen on her travels as a park ranger.

"Maybe you didn't *want* to kill him," she said.

With that, Teach was gone, as if he had never been there. Again, Lisa was left alone, wondering for the second time if what she had seen was real.

Lisa stood on a grassy mountainside overlooking a valley under a clear, blue sky. In the valley was a city, perhaps the largest city she had ever seen, with shiny steel-and-glass buildings that literally seemed to touch the clouds, filling the landscape as far as the eye could see. It could have been any city, anywhere in the world. She could see roads and bridges full of automobiles and huge jetliners making their way above the skyline to unknown destinations. Though Lisa lived in the country, she had always loved the city, with its busy streets and crowds of people going about their daily lives, interacting and communicating with one another about business, about love, about the future, the past. It excited her. Her life was so mundane compared to theirs, or so she had always believed.

"Well, what do you think?"

The voice startled her and she turned to see who stood behind her. It was Teach. Lisa looked down at her clothes and found that she was no longer dressed in jeans, but in a long, flowing white dress made of silk and lace. Probably worth a fortune, she thought. She also noticed she was barefoot.

"Well?" Teach repeated.

Lisa looked up, saw that he wore all black leather. It fit his personality, Lisa thought. She also thought about Teach's glowing charisma. Captivating, like a movie star, something that hadn't really crossed her mind before. Not at all something she really wanted to think about.

"Well, *what?*" she said.

Teach took a few steps in her direction. "What do you think of the city?"

Lisa turned back and looked at the scene once again, then glanced back at Teach. "It's beautiful. And so is this," she said, indicating the dress.

Teach nodded. "I thought you might like it. I had it made especially for you. I must say it fits perfectly . . . in all the right places."

Teach stopped only inches away.

Lisa could smell the musky scent of his breath. His black hair blew around his face in the light mountain breeze. She could see tiny red ribbons braided into his black beard. She felt dizzy and disoriented, like she was in a freefall. An intense wave of moist heat radiated through her belly and breasts, an exquisite feeling. She floated, on the brink of an orgasm. How was this possible? How could a walking dead man give her so much pleasure? Lisa knew she had to be strong here. She knew she couldn't surrender to his blatant seduction.

"So why did you bring me here?" she asked, trying to slow his advances. "Is this a dream, or is this all real?"

Teach smiled and Lisa found it disarming. "Both," he said.

Teach reached up a hand and smoothed Lisa's hair back from her brow. She didn't try to stop him.

"I've never met a woman like you. You make me feel things, do things to me that I don't understand. But I want to understand."

Lisa looked into Teach's eyes, but said nothing. He reached down and put a hand on each of her shoulders, turned her back towards the city and its spectacular view. Lisa found herself mesmerized by its strange, hypnotic beauty. The chaotic sound of it was like music, with a driving, sensual rhythm that thrilled her.

Then Teach leaned down and whispered in her ear, his breath hot upon her neck, causing her to shiver.

"This can all be yours, Lisa. All of it. I will give you the world and, in return, all I ask for is your loyalty. In time, you will learn to love me."

Lisa turned to look at Teach, considering his words, letting them rattle through her mind like balls on a pool table. His pupils were green, yet bright like stained glass, as if fire blazed through them from behind.

Without warning, he leaned down and kissed her, more gently than she ever thought possible. It felt good, and that frightened her. In spite of the fear, she could feel the heat rising up inside her, and she turned to face Teach, slowly falling to her knees before him. She could see the bulge of his erection and thought about how good it would feel inside of her.

But something stopped her. As she was staring at Teach, she quickly closed her eyes as tightly as she could and began whispering over and over again, "No, no, no, no, no, no, no, no!"

She put her hands up to her ears and pressed her palms down on them, blocking out the sound of the city that beckoned to her from the valley.

"I don't have to do this. It's a dream, it's *my* dream!"

She kept her eyes shut for several more seconds, concentrating her mind on one thing, willing herself to be strong, to not give in to temptation.

Slowly, Lisa lowered her hands and opened her eyes.

Hunter stood before her in a faded pair of blue jeans and an old T-shirt, smiling the same sweet smile that always made her melt.

Lisa nodded, as if this latest vision was acceptable, and smiled back at the man of her dreams.

"That's better," she said.

Just after dawn, fishing boats, Coast Guard cutters, and leisure craft started making their way to and fro in the busy Miami port as the *Gertrude* headed back out to sea. After refueling and taking on potable water, Hunter grabbed a quick shower and ate a bowl of stale corn flakes without milk for breakfast. Luckily, there was still enough coffee left to make a fresh pot, which he did. He took a sip and made a face as the strong brew took its toll on his sluggish brain, then went to meet Summerfield in the pilothouse.

Sometime during the night, Hunter had taken his turn at the helm, marveling at the maneuverability of the boat. The vessel practically sailed itself. In fact, with the autopilot switched on, it did drive itself. He had little to do but sit back and watch the waves go by and gaze at the stars. He also kept his eye on the GPS tracker, imagining the little dot to be Lisa, willing the boat to go faster, then reminding himself of the virtue of patience.

Hunter glanced at Summerfield. The sun glinted off his blond mane, accentuating his sharp features and reminding him of some Norse god. Summerfield's skin was tanned nearly as dark as his own, and his khaki pants and button-down shirt were the epitome of preppy. With Summerfield's wealth and youthful good looks, Hunter understood what a young college girl like Lisa might have seen in him. Summerfield even had a decent personality, if a little bookish.

Hunter began to once again feel the pangs of jealousy and quickly shook it off.

Summerfield looked at him and smiled. "Well, we're making pretty good time. Weather report says all the storms are staying off to the east, so it should be smooth sailing. As long as we don't meet up with a giant squid or a killer sperm whale, that is."

Hunter smirked at Summerfield's literary humor and nodded his head.

"Right, Captain Ahab. Or, should I just call you Ishmael?"

Summerfield returned his attention to the open water ahead, his mood seeming to darken. "Maybe you can just call me *crazy*."

"Why do you say that?"

Summerfield shook his head slowly, shrugging his shoulders. "I don't know. This whole adventure is crazy. I mean, here we are heading out into the middle of the Atlantic—"

"Caribbean," Hunter interrupted.

"—Right, Caribbean . . . with nothing to go on but a hunch. I could be wrong about this whole thing, you know."

Hunter thought for a minute, sipping his coffee, looking off into the blue horizon. "You're not wrong. I know you're not . . . *we're* not. Especially after the things we've seen. Nothing human could have made me move across the floor like that, or picked me up by the throat with one hand. As much myth as there is surrounding Blackbeard, I know he was once human, but now he has superhuman strength. Whatever he is now, he's changed, acquired powers beyond those of a man. The fact that he's even alive proves that."

Summerfield nodded, seeming to accept this. "Maybe it's just me, then."

Hunter glanced at his friend. "Having doubts about our mission?"

"Mission? Is that what this is?"

"What else would you call it?"

Summerfield frowned and adjusted the wheel, keeping to the right and maintaining their heading out of the harbor. "Not doubts, necessarily. Just reservations. Reservations about bringing you into all this. And Lisa. I feel bad that you both had the chance to finally reconcile your differences and now . . . well . . . now you've been forced apart."

Hunter smiled and took another drink of coffee. "Believe me, there's no force in the universe that will keep us apart, at least as far as I'm concerned. I'd follow her to the ends of the earth, if that's what it takes. I'll even fight demons."

Now it was Summerfield's turn to smile as he focused his attention on the sea ahead. The boat picked up speed and the engines thrummed as water sprayed up in a roostertail from beneath the stern. They rocked gently from side to side and bounced from wave to wave like a flat stone skimming the water's surface.

"I'm sure you'll have your chance to do just that," Summerfield told him.

Caesar and Jonathan sat in the pilothouse of Aiden's yacht as Jonathan piloted the boat and nursed a cup of lukewarm coffee. He wished he and his grandfather could have been fishing, or something other than what they were doing: accompanying a madman, or *two* madmen, on a journey to nowhere.

Or to Hell.

Down below, Teach sat watching TV and soaking up everything he could about the new world he found himself suddenly thrust into. Jonathan found the demon-man's curiosity amusing, his ability to learn and remember new things frightening. He wondered what the pirate would eventually try to do with Lisa, and hoped that he would be able to somehow stop it. Those thoughts slowly morphed into fantasies of Lisa and Jonathan together, sitting in the cabin below, staring into each other's eyes, he caressing her face, her hair, telling her it would be all right.

A smile crept up on Jonathan's face before he was snapped back to reality by his grandfather's voice.

"A penny for your thoughts."

Jonathan blinked. "Believe me, you don't want to know what I was thinking."

Caesar smiled slyly. "She's spoken for, my son, and by more than one man. I don't think Teach is going to let her go that easily, not even to return to her own husband. She's a very brave woman, that one, to do what she did. Offer herself in his place. Hunter is a lucky man."

Jonathan slowly nodded in agreement. "And she's beautiful."

Caesar smiled slyly. "Forget it. You'll be better off."

Jonathan watched as the early-morning sun crept up

over the eastern horizon. "Caesar, tell me why this is happening. Why, after three-hundred years, has Teach decided that now is the time to return, to find this magical book. There has to be something more here that we're not seeing, something that we're missing. How could he have simply willed himself out of the grave, from under tons of water and sand at the bottom of the ocean? It just doesn't make sense."

Caesar's smile faded as he digested the question, one he knew was bound to come from his hyper-observant grandson. He did his best to frame an answer. "Remember the dreams, Jonathan? Those were not just coincidence. They came from him."

Jonathan couldn't argue with his grandfather. He knew it was true.

"The Death Defier was also known by other names besides Diablero and Obeah. He is also called the Nightmare Walker. He walks in our dreams, sends us thoughts while we sleep, even shapes them to his own. And we are none the wiser."

"Even from beyond the dead?"

Caesar blew out a quick breath of exasperation. "Dead? What is death for one who does not know death?"

Jonathan considered Caesar's words, and kept listening.

"Someone else is involved, a person we have yet to discover. Someone called him up from the dead, probably in hopes of finding the treasure, or maybe even the book itself."

Jonathan stared dumbfounded at Caesar, wondering if his grandfather knew about the bottle and scroll they had found inside the *Adventure*. But he doubted it.

"You're telling me there is someone following us, or watching us, someone who is hoping to find Blackbeard's treasure?"

"Since the day I first felt the presence of Blackbeard—of the demon that possesses him—I understood there was another force behind him, that he could not have risen by his own power. It is the work of someone who understands Vodun, or a similar religion. Someone who was able to cast a spell to empower the demon to reanimate the bones of Blackbeard. That is why I called you, told you about the demon. I need your help to stop him. I am too old to do it alone."

"But who besides you would have such power? Who would know the ways of Vodun in the United States that could perform such a feat?"

Caesar shrugged and smiled. "The world of mysticism is not restricted to one man, my son. It can be accessed by anyone who has the will and the perseverance to do so, and the mind to understand."

Jonathan wondered exactly how much his grandfather knew, and how much he was telling. "Why hasn't Blackbeard spoken to you, other than the time at the house? According to the history books, you were inseparable from the time you joined his crew."

Caesar sighed heavily. "Teach was my friend, but he was a man. He had the feelings and desires and heart of a man. A demon has a heart of evil and its desires go beyond that of mortals. It craves power, the power of immortality, because it knows it has but a short time. Any time it can gain upon this Earth is worth any price. So, you see, things like friendship and loyalty no longer have any meaning to him. He exists only to fulfill his desires. The ultimate narcissist, you might say."

Jonathan nodded, trying to imagine living without the need for love or friendship, and found that the thought of it made him profoundly sad. He wondered if that was how it felt to be a demon, cast into darkness for all eternity, knowing there was no hope but that which could be temporarily gained from possession of an earthly body. Was that how the Death Defier felt?

Jonathan stood and stretched his arms above his head, trying to keep above the black lake of despair and hopelessness the discussion with his grandfather had brought on. He swayed slightly, balancing himself, trying to gain his sea legs as the boat rocked back and forth and side to side in the water. He turned toward the bow, looked out across the waves scanning the horizon.

A boat approached from well off in the distance.

Jonathan blinked and rubbed the sea spray out of his eyes. There was definitely a boat on the horizon.

He reached under the console and pulled out a pair of binoculars, and glassed the approaching vessel. Sea water sprayed up from the boat's stern, and Jonathan estimated it to be doing about thirty knots. It seemed to be heading straight for them, and there were several dark-skinned men aboard. He didn't like the looks of it. They were miles out from Miami and a mayday call would take too long for the Coast Guard to answer. Their only hope was to pray that the men on the boat weren't pirates. Though Aiden did have guns on board, thanks to his paranoia, they would be no match for a gang of organized criminals.

Caesar watched with mild interest, seemingly unperturbed by Jonathan's sudden intensity. "Pirates?" he asked.

Jonathan looked at him. "I don't know. They might be. Or maybe they're just curious. It's hard to say. They'll be on us in another couple of minutes, though, and the question will be academic. In the meantime, I suggest we do whatever we can to prepare."

Caesar laughed, surprising Jonathan. "And do what? Hit them with cannon fire? We're on a yacht, my son. We have no defenses other than a couple of pistols, and I would be willing to bet they would be no match against the high-tech weapons they are likely carrying."

Jonathan stared blankly at his grandfather, momentarily at a loss for words, then said, "Well, what would you suggest we do? Throw up our hands and surrender? They would probably kill us, and God only knows what they will do when they find we have a beautiful woman on board."

Caesar held his solemn gaze, as if waiting for Jonathan to finish his rant. Jonathan's annoyance at his grandfather was building. Several choice words formed in his mind, but he held his tongue.

"There is only one thing we can do," Caesar said.

Jonathan crossed his arms. "And what, pray tell, is that?"

"Call Blackbeard."

"Blackbeard?"

"Yes. Call him to the main deck and tell him what is happening. Then I suggest the rest of us go below. Things may get ugly very quickly."

Jonathan shook his head, then raised his binoculars and took another look at the oncoming boat. It looked very much like Aiden's boat, but smaller and more aerodynamic. Obviously built for speed and maneuverability, as opposed to leisure. All the better for chasing down its quarry, Jonathan thought.

As he watched, he saw the men simultaneously reach behind their heads and pull something down over their faces.

Masks. They were all wearing black ski masks. They reached down to the deck and picked up weapons—some pistols and what looked like semiautomatic or automatic rifles.

"They're definitely pirates. Several of them, and they're not coming to have coffee. They're well armed with automatic weapons."

Caesar, unflustered, remained in his seat.

Jonathan looked over at him and shook his head. "Don't you care that we're about to be raided, or worse?"

Caesar's smile faded, but he remained calm. "Of course I'm concerned, but there is no weapon better than the one we have below deck. His name is Edward Teach. Now go and call him."

Caesar's words finally took hold. Jonathan turned and looked behind them at the ladder leading down to the galley. He smiled at Caesar. "I'll be right back. Can you take the helm?"

Caesar rose from his seat and looked at the big teakwood steering wheel. He nodded at Jonathan. "Be glad to."

In less than a minute, Blackbeard was climbing up to the pilothouse, Jonathan close behind. Blackbeard stopped beside him and looked out over the bow. "Are those the pirates?" he asked simply.

Caesar looked at the approaching boat, now almost upon them. "Yes. There are several men with guns. I fear they will try to board us and possibly steal the boat, maybe even kill us."

As he spoke, Aiden came up the ladder, then Lisa. They stood in the background, watching as the boat drew near.

"What the hell's going on? Don't tell me we have more pirates to deal with," Lisa said.

Jonathan turned and looked at the pair. "Look, these people are extremely dangerous, so I suggest we all get down below decks while we can. Let's go."

He held out his arms and ushered all of them—with the exception of Blackbeard—back down the steps and into the galley.

Blackbeard eyed the yacht's throttle and steering wheel, then grabbed the throttle and gradually began to slow the boat until it came to a complete stop. That should make it easier for them, he thought.

The pirate speedboat came up alongside and a couple of masked men pulled the two boats close with long grappling hooks, then tied them together with thick nylon rope.

Teach heard the men speak, and realized he understood the language. Haitian.

He grinned broadly as one of the men climbed over the side and advanced toward him. The man kept a sleek, black AK-47 assault rifle trained on Teach's skull.

"I am going to feast on your blood, and then I will devour your souls," Teach said in perfect Haitian Creole.

The Haitian pirates stood on the bow of the boat as it bobbed up and down in the water, watching in stunned silence as Teach began removing his clothes.

The four of them, Jonathan, Caesar, Aiden and Lisa, huddled together in the yacht's center sleeping area, the one currently in use by Jonathan and Caesar, and prayed that the pirates had not seen them, or were at least too preoccupied to bother looking.

At first, they could hear the footfalls of the men from the other boat as they boarded the yacht, then silence, followed by shouts of alarm, an inhuman, bellowing roar, automatic weapon fire, and screaming.

They all knew what the screaming meant—Blackbeard had changed and was now likely ripping them limb from limb. Jonathan looked over at his grandfather and saw that his eyes had became glazed and his lips moved slightly, unintelligible words forming upon them. The demon had once again pulled him into its mind and now Caesar was seeing everything it was seeing, like a camera, watching, but helpless to take any action of his own.

Jonathan was curious, more so than the others. He had to know, had to see exactly what Teach had become. He elbowed his way through the group and put his hand on the door knob.

"Where the hell do you think you're going? You'll give us away if you go out there." Lisa's loud whisper was full of venom, and she sounded as if she were ready to strike if Jonathan so much as flinched.

Jonathan glanced back at her. "Believe me, those pirates have more to worry about than us. They're too preoccupied to be bothered about anything other than killing that demon. Besides, I have to see him, I have to know what it looks like."

Lisa's eyes seemed to soften a little, but she refused to

budge. Jonathan tried a different tact.

"Aren't you the least bit curious? Don't you want to know?"

Though she didn't want to admit it, Lisa knew he was right and was just as curious as Jonathan. Whatever unnatural animal Teach had become, Lisa had to see it. She began to move towards the door.

Caesar seemed unconcerned, but Aiden watched with dismay as the two slowly opened the door and stepped out into the galley, then turned and gazed through the windows overlooking the boat's main deck.

What they saw looked like something out of Dante's Hell. Blood and body parts were scattered across the deck like pieces of a ghastly jigsaw puzzle, glistening dark red in the sun. Bits of tattered and torn cloth and guns were added to the mix, some with the fingers of severed hands still on their triggers.

And in the midst of it, a huge, steel-muscled four-legged creature covered in black fur advanced on the remaining gunman, who fired every round of his AK-47, to no effect. The bullets were no more than an annoyance to the demon, whose skin swallowed them and healed over as if it had never been penetrated. The pair watched in horror and lurid fascination as the animal stalked the man, who finally turned and jumped back over the side and onto his own boat. He attempted to untie the two vessels, dropping his useless gun into the water and fumbling with the knots, but Lisa and Jonathan knew there would be no escape.

The sudden leap of the creature onto the other boat startled the pair, and they watched as the man backed away from it, turned to dive in the water, and was caught from behind by an oversized hand-paw. The creature held the Haitian in the air, turned him around and looked into his eyes, reveling in the fear, and Jonathan and Lisa could see it bare huge fangs, still moist with the blood of its victims. Then it was upon the man, rending and tearing him to pieces so quickly that the Haitian pirate did not even have time to scream.

Jonathan and Lisa looked at one another, then back at the carnage, and wondered if coming out of the berthing compartment had been such a good idea.

Jonathan's mouth felt like it was full of cotton.

"Jesus," he said, as much a prayer as it was an exclamation.

When the beast had finished its gruesome task, it lumbered to the starboard side of the other boat and leaped over to the yacht with surprisingly feline grace. Yet they could see, now that the creature was closer, that it was neither feline nor canine, but a mix of the two. It also resembled a bear in the shape of its head and its pointed ears, but the musculature was more well-defined, the fur not quite as dense as that of a bear. A were-bear-wolf was the only description Jonathan could think of. The yacht actually dipped under its weight as it moved across the deck towards them. The deep rumbling breaths the beast took as it walked reminded Jonathan of an angry rhino, or the snorting of a bull. He could also see, with mild disgust, the creature's huge member swinging back and forth between its legs like an oversized salami.

Then it stopped in front of the window directly before them, and bared its yellow fangs, looking more like a grin than a snarl, as if it was proud of itself. He could see pieces of skin and cloth still stuck to the teeth, and Jonathan knew that its breath likely smelled of human flesh and coppery blood; he started to feel queasy. Its eyes were as red as burning embers, and Jonathan felt them boring into him. A cold bead of sweat trickled down his forehead.

He looked over at Lisa, who was now watching him with a furrowed brow, and began to say something.

Instead, Jonathan passed out.

"We're about two hours out from New Providence," Summerfield said.

Hunter sat in his chair and nodded absentmindedly, staring off into the distance with one foot propped on the console and one hand on his chin.

Summerfield looked over at him. "The Thinker," he said with a smirk.

Hunter looked up at him. "Huh?"

"The Thinker . . . you know, Rodin's sculpture representing Dante at the gates of Hell."

Hunter nodded slowly. "That's appropriate. I feel like we're approaching the gates of Hell right about now."

Jason turned back toward the horizon. "Maybe we are."

Hunter returned to his thinking pose. "I just can't seem to figure out something, though."

"What's that?"

"How did Blackbeard, after nearly three centuries under the ocean, manage to bring himself back to life? It seems to me that he might have had some outside help, someone who knew the legend. Someone who knew that he was possessed by a demon and who knew where to find the skull."

"I don't think any of that was really a secret. Blackbeard often spent his time boasting about being in league with the Devil. I mean, look at his flag—a demon holding an hourglass and a spear. It's just that most people thought he was only bluffing, making his persona more terrifying in order to frighten his potential victims."

"Yeah, but there's someone involved here who knows more than your average pirate buff; someone who knows how to raise people from the dead and how to control demons. I don't think that's something you can learn from Wikipedia. And I sure don't think Blackbeard did it himself."

"So, who do you have in mind?"

"Jonathan."

"Jonathan? Caesar's son? But why would he want to raise Blackbeard from the dead?"

"Why else? Greed, the need for power and riches. Can you imagine finding Blackbeard's treasure? You would likely be the next Bill Gates. Plus, he's an archeologist. That's what he does. He's like a corrupt version of Indiana Jones. And his own grandfather is a shaman. I mean, it all adds up. In fact, they might be in it together."

Summerfield slowly began nodding his head. "I see what you mean. You make a good case. I still can't believe Caesar would be involved in something like that, though. He's always been a pretty stand-up guy. I think he could have been rich long ago if he had been so inclined."

"Maybe he doesn't know. Maybe it's all a setup to get him to cast the spell in that book and make the demon stronger so Jonathan can use it for his own purposes."

"You think he would do that to his own grandfather?"

"In a heartbeat."

Summerfield shrugged. "Well, what do I know? Maybe you're right."

Hunter sat up and put his feet down on the deck. "The main thing I'm worried about is what they're doing to Lisa on that boat. I mean, you have a shaman, a thief, a demon, and that little weird guy with the gun on board a yacht headed for Voodoo country. For all I know, they could be preparing her for a sacrifice."

"If I remember correctly, they usually require virgins for that purpose."

"So far as you know. Those may be hard to come by in this day and age."

"I wouldn't worry too much. Caesar would be unlikely to let anything happen to her. Besides, she can pretty well take care of herself, don't you think?"

Hunter nodded, stood and took a deep breath, closed his eyes, and began raising his arms then lowering them to his sides. Summerfield watched with amused interest as Hunter's movements became more complex, as if performed in response to some unheard symphony. His arms and legs moved like the hands of a clock from position to position with the power and grace of a trained dancer. This went on for several minutes until, at last, Summerfield could no longer contain his curiosity.

"May I ask exactly what it is you're doing?"

Hunter stopped his movements. "Don't tell me you've never done Tai Chi."

"Oh, is that what that is? I thought maybe you were trying to fly or . . ."

Summerfield's retort was cut off as Hunter's eyes grew narrow, spotting something on the horizon. He turned toward the bow and saw an object floating in the distance.

Hunter said, "Hey, do you have a telescope or some binoculars?"

Summerfield slowed the boat to a stop, then lifted up the seat of the captain's chair. Underneath was a hidden cache of weapons and ammunition. He looked up at Hunter. "Hey, always be prepared, I say."

Hunter smirked. "Since when does a Boy Scout carry a gun?"

Summerfield handed the binoculars to Hunter. "Who said I was a Boy Scout?"

Hunter raised the glasses to his eyes, observing the object. He saw a large powerboat listing to port, and what appeared to be an arm limply hanging over the side. Several fins circled the boat. Likely sharks.

Hunter lowered the binoculars and handed them back to Summerfield.

"Well," Hunter said, "it definitely looks like our boy

has been through here. He doesn't even bother to cover his tracks. That should tell you just how contemptuous he is of our ability to stop him."

Jonathan woke up on his back in his stateroom, rubbed his eyes and saw Caesar on one side of the bed and Lisa on the other. He also felt a large knot on the front of his head, likely where he had knocked it on the wooden deck when he passed out. The intense pain nauseated him.

Caesar, as usual, held a large grin on his face. "You're lucky you don't have a concussion. You fainted like a frightened schoolgirl," he said.

Jonathan groaned as he rubbed his head and tried to sit up. "I never could stand the sight of blood, especially when it's dripping from the jaws of a demon. Did you see that thing?" Slowly, he dropped his feet over the side of the bed and sat with shoulders hunched, looking down at the floor for several minutes as he tried to regain his composure.

Lisa cleared her throat. "Well, I guess you're not the he-man you make yourself out to be."

Jonathan looked up at Lisa blankly, then turned his gaze back to the floor in defeat.

"Don't worry, your secret's safe with me," she said.

As if on cue, both Aiden and Blackbeard appeared in the stateroom doorway. Teach, dressed in all black and looking every bit the part of his infamous persona, eyed the group in the room one at a time, stopping at Caesar. "We're getting very close to San Salvador. Anyone thinking of trying to escape should understand the consequences after witnessing the fate of those unfortunate Haitian pirates."

Teach let the words sink in as a faint smile played across his lips.

Jonathan didn't want to seem as if he were gushing, but the power the demon possessed boggled his mind. He would likely never meet anyone like Teach again. Jonathan was first and foremost a scientist. A very curious scientist. "Captain Teach," he started, unsure of what to call the man. "Mr. Blackbeard . . . how do you do that? Change into other life forms like that? Make things move on their own? I mean—it's, it's—well, it's fucking amazing. Does that book really give a person *that* kind of power?"

Everyone in the room stared at Jonathan and then at Blackbeard. Jonathan felt like an idiot.

Teach eyed Jonathan, but said nothing, then turned and left with Aiden following close behind like an obedient puppy.

Jonathan looked from the doorway back up at Lisa. "You know, those two make a fine couple—Yin and Yang—except I think they're both Yang."

Lisa nodded in agreement. "They definitely have some kind of connection. It's too convenient that Aiden somehow got accidentally involved in all this. It seems planned, as if it was meant to happen this way."

Caesar chuckled, and Lisa and Jonathan both looked over at him.

Lisa crossed her arms. "What's so funny? I'd like to know so I can laugh, too."

Caesar shook his head slowly. "We're just puppets and Blackbeard is pulling the strings. It has always been that way, even when he was a pirate. And whoever is in cahoots with him is being used as well, though likely they don't know it yet. And when he is done with them . . ." Caesar drew a finger across his throat to make his point.

Jonathan shook his head. "That's a sobering thought."

"And to answer your question," Caesar continued, glancing at his grandson, "it's not just the book. The demon gives him the power to do the things he does. He is the Death Defier, the Shape Shifter, the—"

"I know, the Nightmare Walker," Jonathan finished.

Lisa turned and looked out the portal, saw the shore beginning to draw closer. But they seemed to be out of sight of any harbor, or even another boat. The sun shone under a bright blue sky and would have been exhilarating under other circumstances, she thought.

She turned back to the old shaman. "Caesar, have you ever been here before?"

Caesar shrugged. "Maybe, maybe not. It's been so long. I seem to remember something about it. A lot of the pirates came here to escape the watchful eyes of the Royal Navy and to hide their treasure. I know Captain Blackbeard hid some things here, some gold coins and wine casks we plundered from French vessels, probably other things. But I do know that the book is here, somewhere, and only Teach knows where. He was alone when he hid it. It was the one thing he wished to keep completely to himself. After I foolishly gave it to him, that is."

Jonathan got up off the bed and stood, feeling a little unsteady. He reached out to Lisa and she grabbed his hand. They stared at each other for a brief moment, caught off guard by the sudden contact, like a small jolt of electricity. Lisa felt her cheeks flush and let go, and Jonathan turned to the door.

"Well, let's go up and see what there is to see," he said.

Summerfield and Hunter watched the GPS signal. They were approaching one of the outer islands, beyond New Providence. The area looked like it hadn't been inhabited for quite some time. They could see the shoreline—bleached-white sand thick with palm trees and underbrush. Crystal clear water. Colorful tropical fish, sea urchins, even a small sea turtle.

Summerfield steered the yacht, and prayed that they were following the same route to shore that Lisa and her captors had taken.

Then, they saw the boat. It was huge, two decks with a pilothouse on top. As sleek and modern as any boat Hunter had ever seen. Its bow was facing forward, as if it was prepared to get underway quickly.

And it was unoccupied.

He glanced sideways at Summerfield. "Looks like they took off already. Are we still tracking them?"

Summerfield glanced at the GPS indicator. "So far, so good. I think they're moving inland, away from the beach."

"Where the hell are we, anyway? I thought you said they were heading to New Providence. This is one of the outer islands."

Summerfield shrugged. He reached under the console and pulled out an old, well-worn map, then opened it up and ran his finger across it. After a few seconds of searching, he looked over at Hunter. "I think this is Cat Island, named after Arthur Catt. Most believe it was discovered by Columbus and named San Salvador, until they eventually changed it back to Cat Island."

"Who was Arthur Catt?"

"A pirate. Likely a contemporary of you-know-who.

Legend has it that Catt frequented the island, so I wouldn't be surprised that Blackbeard knew about it."

"Figures. It's a beautiful place, though. Any other time, I'd probably like it here."

"I hope you're not afraid of heights—this island has the highest elevation in the chain—206 feet above sea level."

Hunter glanced at Summerfield, marveling at his friend's deadpan sense of humor in this tense situation. "Funny," he said.

As the pair drew closer to Aiden's boat, they could see it was tied to a small, ancient pier, boards and pylons rotting and covered with white seagull droppings. Hunter also noticed something else. The main deck of the boat was covered with dried blood and sported a couple of bullet holes.

Summerfield whistled. "Must have been a massacre on board."

Hunter said, "More than likely the people on that boat we saw a ways back. Probably pirates. Blackbeard obviously didn't see them as kindred spirits."

Summerfield reversed the boat's propellers, slowing their momentum and allowing them to gently slip in next to the pier. As they drew close, Hunter leaped over the side onto the slimy wood, nearly slipping, then caught his balance. Holding the nylon rope from a cleat on the bow of the boat, he quickly moved aft and tied the boat off to the pier. He jumped back onto the boat and grabbed another nylon rope from the stern and tied this one off near the forward part of the boat, effectively crisscrossing the ropes. He looked up to Summerfield and gave the thumbs up, and heard the twin engines slow to idle, then stop.

The silence was eerie. Hunter glanced into the jungle and saw an open path leading through the undergrowth.

Summerfield climbed over the side of the boat to join him. "Well, my guess is they went through there," Summerfield said, pointing to the opening.

Hunter glanced at him. "Brilliant, Sherlock. That would have been my guess, too."

Summerfield smiled and shrugged. Hunter noticed a bulge beneath his shirt, near the waistband of his pants.

"Are you packing?"

Summerfield winked. "Of course."

Hunter nodded. "Let's go."

The path through the jungle wasn't nearly as clear as they had hoped. Hunter found himself wishing he had a machete to chop through some of the thick foliage. Brambles, vines, and thorny bushes crossed the path, impeding their progress and making Hunter all the more frustrated. The vines were so thick, they managed to create a canopy in the trees above, effectively blocking out much of the afternoon sunlight. In the distance, a woodpecker chipped away at a tree, and he could hear the *wichety wich* of a Bahama Yellowthroat. Unfortunately, Hunter was not in the mood at the moment to appreciate the animal life of Cat Island.

A large mosquito landed on Hunter's arm and he slapped it, leaving a speck of blood on his skin. "How the hell did they get through this stuff, anyway? It seems like they would have left a path behind them."

Jason thought for a moment. "Obviously, there's another path somewhere, one that's parallel to this one. Either that, or they covered their tracks."

Hunter figured that to be the case. They knew someone would be following them and wanted to slow them down as much as possible.

As Hunter was considering this, the darkness began to diminish and the path became wider, the vines and underbrush less dense.

Soon they were in a clearing. Directly in front of them was a field and in the middle of the field sat a structure about fifty feet long and twenty feet wide. Built entirely of stone, its roof was steepled, and a small cross protruded from the back portion. Along its sides and front were small, square windows set with stained glass. The door, which looked to be hewn from pine, was also inset with stained glass. The building looked as if it was part of the rock upon which it sat. Hunter thought it was probably a Catholic church, or had been at one time. But surrounding the door and below some of the stained-glass windows were symbols, ones which Hunter had never seen before.

He turned to Summerfield. "What do you think those symbols mean?"

Jason shook his head. "I'm not sure, but I think they're Voodoo symbols. There's a lot of that on these islands, especially this one. Many of the people here combined religions from their ancestral homelands with teachings they learned from the Spanish Catholics, effectively creating their own hybrid religions. One of them was Obeah."

"Obeah? As in the Death Defier?"

Summerfield nodded.

Hunter looked back at the symbols. "Nice. I just hope…"

Hunter's words were cut short by a woman's scream from deep inside the church.

They turned to face each other, communicating with their fear-filled eyes.

The scream sounded like Lisa's voice.

Hunter was the first to make a dash for the door of the old church, his white Reeboks making a swishing sound through the tall grass in the open field. Summerfield followed close behind.

They got to the door and found it already open.

Stepping inside, Hunter realized there wasn't much to see. The church looked worse inside than did the exterior. Pews had been splintered and knocked over. The wooden altar had toppled over. Broken glass littered the floor, crunching under their feet as they walked toward the front of the sanctuary.

They stopped before the fallen altar.

In the desolate quiet, Hunter surveyed the building, his head swiveling in a 360-degree sweep. "Damn. I *know* we heard Lisa scream. Where the hell could they be?"

As Hunter spoke, Summerfield tapped his arm, and pointed down at the floor. The place in the floor where the toppled altar had sat had what looked like a trapdoor, large enough for an adult to climb through.

Hunter moved to the trapdoor and found an edge, then lifted the heavy wood and let it crash back to the floor, opening the dark void. The dust of centuries puffed into the air like a mushroom cloud.

Inside was black as pitch and leading ominously down into it was an ancient wooden ladder.

Summerfield glanced at Hunter. "You know what? I'm going to the boat to grab a flashlight. Don't do anything until I get back."

Hunter nodded absentmindedly, staring down into the dark pit as if it might suddenly come alive and pull him inside, as it had likely done to Lisa.

He watched as Summerfield ran out the door, glass crunching under his shoes. Then, he moved to the hole and took a step onto the ladder's first rung.

Hunter climbed down into the abyss. The ladder, which seemed sturdy, felt as if it was covered in cold slime. He figured it was probably the sweat of his own hands. He had decided that waiting for Summerfield to return with a flashlight wasn't an option. Lisa was in trouble and needed him now. He only prayed he wasn't too late.

On his descent he was hit with a putrid stench, like a mix of decaying marine growth and animal feces. He hoped it was only temporary.

As he descended, he periodically looked up, saw the entrance becoming smaller. He kept going, continuing down for what seemed like forever. Did this thing have a bottom?

As he looked below, he noticed a faint glow of light. It seemed to be off in the distance. Slowly it dawned on him that not only was the space getting bigger as he descended, but the light he had spotted was moving, like someone walking while carrying either a candle or a flashlight. The ladder now had a slow wobble, caused by its extreme length and his movement.

Out of nowhere, he heard a loud screeching, first one tiny voice, then hundreds. He recognized the sound immediately, having been in several caves in his lifetime, and hid his face from the coming onslaught.

The bats came in waves, relentlessly streaming out of their hiding places far above. Leathery wings smacked against his ears and his back as he held onto the ladder with both arms wrapped tight around the rungs.

As the torrent seemed to taper off, Hunter dared to take a peek up at the roof of the cave.

A lone bat suddenly smacked against the side of Hunter's face. He let out a yelp as he threw his hands up to shield himself.

Then, he was falling.

Lisa couldn't believe what she was seeing. Stone markers and makeshift wooden crosses of hundreds of graves. Holes for the bodies had been carved, with pickaxes, into the limestone floor of the cavern. The graves were covered with stones. In the distance she spotted a sarcophagus and a small mausoleum. The stale air smelled like death.

"What is this place?" Lisa asked.

"It's a graveyard for the followers of Obeah," Caesar said. "They were put here underground to hide from grave robbers and from the government. Some are hundreds of years old, some only a few weeks."

Lisa glanced at Caesar. "But why put them under a church?"

"Can you think of a better place to hide a graveyard?"

Lisa played her flashlight beam across the sea of grave markers and slowly shook her head. "Who is buried here?"

Surprisingly, it was Blackbeard who answered. "Pirates. Many of them members of my crew, killed in battle." Blackbeard looked at Lisa, his eyes glowing red in the darkness of the cave. "Some were women such as you. Fierce warriors, unafraid either of death or of delivering death by cutlass or pistol. They lived and died by my word, and soon, they will live again."

Lisa could hear the fury in Blackbeard's voice, reminding her of the beast she had seen aboard Aiden's yacht only hours before. An involuntary shudder ran down her spine.

As she stared at Teach, Jonathan, who was on her other side, leaned in closely and whispered. "I wonder if Ann Bonney is buried here."

Lisa was puzzled. "Who?"

Jonathan rolled his eyes. "Never mind."

Teach turned back towards the graveyard and began scanning the area, looking for something. He seemed to have no problem seeing in the dark and moved out among the gravestones, as if the cavern was bathed in sunlight. He walked first one way, then another, reading each stone, looking for a name. When he found the grave he was looking for, he knelt on the limestone and began moving the rocks that were piled up inside the hole.

The group watched Teach as they slowly walked to the grave. Aiden stopped in front of the stone, and holding his lantern close, he read the name chiseled there.

His face went slack.

"Oh, my God. I don't believe it. I thought he had gone to London after the pirate trials in Virginia."

Caesar shook his head. "He did, but he returned to Cat Island on a merchant ship to regain his favor with the Obeah. Unfortunately, he died of malaria before he could take advantage of the spell that prolongs life."

Lisa looked at the pair, then at the grave marker. "Who is he?"

Caesar glanced at her. "Israel Hands, Captain Blackbeard's first mate."

Lisa's eyes widened. She shone her light down at the grave stone. *Israel Hands – 1725* was crudely etched upon the headstone. "So what's special about this particular grave?"

Caesar turned to where Blackbeard had uncovered what looked like ancient sailcloth with something inside. "I think we're about to find out."

Suddenly the group heard a cacophonous screeching behind them, like a thousand nails scraping on a blackboard. The horrendous noise was followed by a black cloud swooping down from the cave ceiling and into a lone figure cowering against the ladder.

Bats!

The bats continued on to the other end of the cave, and

after several seconds, all was silent once again.

The man on the ladder let out a yelp, and fell ten or fifteen feet to the floor. It would be a miracle if he weren't impaled on a stalagmite, Lisa thought.

She let out a gasp. "Hunter?" she whispered.

Leaning up against one of the large stalagmites protruding from the limestone floor, Hunter knew how lucky he was to be sitting there unscathed, let alone still alive. Instinctively, he had pulled himself into a ball on the way down, narrowly avoiding impalement.

He wiggled his toes and fingers, then each leg and arm in turn, checking for sprains or broken bones. Amazingly, there were none. He didn't seem to have any bruised ribs, though his butt was sore from the hard landing on the stone floor.

He tried to stand. His legs wobbled slightly and he felt some dizziness, but other than some minor scrapes, he was fine.

"Guess Summerfield won't laugh at my Tai Chi anymore," he mumbled, then turned to try and locate the movement he had seen while hanging precariously from the old ladder. Looking in every direction in the darkness, he noticed some lights in the distance about a hundred yards from where he stood. Hunter thought about calling out, but decided against it. It would be best to maintain anonymity. If they had seen him fall, they probably thought he was injured. Or worse.

Using what little light filtered in from the opening above, he began to move slowly, feeling his way around the stalagmites, stepping cautiously. From research he had done for vacations that he and Lisa had never taken, Hunter knew that many of the primeval forest caves in the Bahamas had pits in them, much like the one he had come down to reach this cave. Those pits might lead to other caves, or could possibly be booby trapped. He knew the only snakes on the islands were small, nonpoisonous boas and racers, but he didn't want to step on one nonetheless, or fall into a pit full of them.

Hunter continued to move inexorably forward, knowing that Lisa's very life may depend on his timeliness. If only he had taken one of Summerfield's guns. He had never particularly liked guns, had seen too many people killed back home on the reservation. But he also believed in the right of self-defense, and right now some blue steel would be quite comforting.

He could hear voices, one female and many male, but couldn't quite make out the words.

"I have to see if he's all right." Lisa fought against Jonathan's iron grip, trying to get back to where she had seen the body fall from the ladder.

Jonathan tried talking some sense into her. "Listen, Lisa, you can't go to him. If he's hurt, then that other guy, Summerstorm—"

"Summer*field*."

"Whatever . . . his friend will take care of him. But if we're going to help, we need to maintain some element of surprise. Understand?"

Jonathan could feel Lisa's arms relax in his grip. He could also hear her quietly sobbing, trying unsuccessfully to gain control of her emotions. He turned her slowly around to face him.

"Look, I know how you feel. But do you think Blackbeard is just going to let you go? He would follow you and then likely kill Hunter and his friend, too."

Lisa slowly nodded her head, wiping her face with the back of her sleeve. Jonathan released his grip.

"Besides, that guy is one tough son of a bitch. I doubt

the fall even hurt him."

Lisa sniffled, a smile creeping up on her face. "You're probably right."

A commotion at the gravesite caused Caesar and Aiden to cry out in surprise.

Jonathan and Lisa moved closer to the grave.

Lisa shone her flashlight on Teach, who held an object in his hand as he rose to stand. She cast her light to the ground, and saw that inside the shallow hole lay the skeletal remains of Israel Hands. What remained of the corpse's dusty, brittle clothes covered the dry bones. And in the weak light, Lisa spied black eye sockets and grinning, yellow teeth.

Looking back at Teach, she saw his eyes light up as if he had just discovered the Holy Grail. He held a book in his huge hands. She knew by looking at it that it was the book they had been seeking.

One thing that disturbed Lisa was the physical appearance of the book's cover. Like the fictional Necronomicon, or Book of the Dead, the cover was made of human skin. In fact, it was a face, stretched hideously out of proportion to cover the book. The skin had obviously been treated somehow, like tanning leather, to keep it from rotting over the centuries and to protect what was inside from the elements. The eyes were closed and the mouth was contorted in agony, as if its owner had protested, but to no avail.

Lisa stifled a scream, closing her eyes against the horrific sight.

Teach turned back toward the far side of the cave and continued on, leaving the grave open. Lisa felt almost as if it were sacrilegious to leave the grave defiled, with Israel Hands laying there open to the elements and to the eyes of the living. But she held her tongue. The group reluctantly followed Teach, and after a few dozen yards, Jonathan could see they had come to a dead end. They stopped, shining their lights on the wall.

Jonathan let out a sigh. "Great. Now what do we do?"

Teach reached out to the wall and touched a single stone that seemed to be embedded there. To everyone's surprise, the stone sunk into a hole and the wall began to move.

"Holy shit!" Jonathan exclaimed. "What happened?"

Caesar's eyes were wide with astonishment. "I don't remember this place."

Blackbeard turned to him. "That's because I didn't want you to remember," he growled.

The wall, which had looked to be solid, was actually a large stone wheel, and the group could see it as they shone their flashlights around its outer edges. It slowly rolled sideways on the other side of the wall, revealing a dark passage.

Jonathan squinted, trying to make out whether the faint glow he saw coming from within was actually there, or only his imagination.

"You know, I could be wrong, but I think I see light coming from inside."

Blackbeard held up his lantern and stepped through the opening.

"You're not wrong," he said.

"To tell you the truth, I don't really want to go in there," Lisa said to no one in particular, eyeing the passage through which Teach had just disappeared.

Jonathan held up his lantern and peered through the opening. "I'd have to agree with you on that one. This place is already creepy enough without secret passageways."

As they stood deciding what to do next, Aiden made up their minds for them. "Go on and step through. Blackbeard is waiting for us."

Jonathan, Caesar, and Lisa whirled around and saw Aiden aiming his nine-millimeter Glock in their direction, his wild eyes gleaming in the lantern light.

Caesar glanced at his companions, all of whom looked to be in shock. "Well, I guess he means business. Let's go."

The echo of their footsteps on the cavern's floor sounded hollow and much too loud as they made their way down the passage. Jonathan, who had spent many years in caves both underwater and underground, held his light close to the walls, inspecting its surface. "It looks as if these walls are man-made," he mused. "It doesn't have the rough, uneven texture of the walls in most primeval forest caves. Somebody dug this passage by hand."

Just as Jonathan had finished speaking, the group came upon another smaller chamber, adjacent to the one they had just left. It was a room about the size of a large house, nearly rectangular in shape and devoid of cracks, crevices, stalagmites, or stalactites. There were no vines or tree roots growing from the ceiling or the walls, which were as smooth as polished stone.

In the center of the room was a primitive altar, which seemed to grow out of the cave floor. The altar was covered with small, wax candles, and beside it stood two shadowy figures. One of them was Blackbeard; the other was someone none of them had seen before. The group turned and looked at one another, then back at the dark pair.

Lisa was the first to speak to their new guest. "Um . . . who the hell are you?"

The man was dark-skinned, likely a native of the island, and wore only a simple robe. His hair hung in long dreadlocks, and when he grinned, Lisa saw that his teeth were all capped in gold crowns. He was an older man, maybe mid-fifties, and he looked frail. He stood with his fingers interlocked, as if he were a professor about to give a lecture to a class of undergraduates. The grin he wore was decidedly malevolent.

The man gave Lisa the creeps.

"I can see why Captain Blackbeard has chosen you," he said. "You have a lot of spirit."

Lisa's eyes filled with fire and her cheeks became flushed. "Nobody has chosen me, you old—"

Before she could finish her sentence, Jonathan grabbed her arm and whispered harshly into her ear. "Not now. This isn't the time."

Lisa glanced at Jonathan, barely able to contain her rage, but she realized he was right. At the moment, there was nothing she, or any of them, could do about their situation.

"We have waited a very long time for this day, have we not, my friend?" the old man said to Blackbeard.

Jonathan, who had been to the Bahamas many times, thought it strange that the man spoke with a slight English accent. The old priest, or whatever he was, did not seem to speak with inflections common to the small chain of islands—a mix of Shakespearian English, African, and local island dialect.

As they watched the old man, his eyes seemed to

momentarily roll back in his head, then quickly return to normal. "It also seems we have another visitor. Mr. Aiden, please help our friend find his way."

Aiden turned and disappeared through the passageway. Moments later, a figure came into view, followed by Aiden and his ever-present Glock.

Lisa sucked in her breath as she eyed Hunter being led into the clearing.

Hunter walked into the chamber. Lisa threw herself into his arms, kissing him with all the passion she could muster under the circumstances.

He reached into his pocket and pulled out the silver cross necklace, then gently placed it around her neck. "You dropped this," he said.

"I thought you were dead," she whispered breathlessly.

Hunter held Lisa at arm's length, looking intently into her eyes. "So did I. We heard you scream. Are you okay?"

"Scream? Oh, yeah. The bats."

Hunter pulled Lisa toward him and looked around the room, nodding in turn at Jonathan and Caesar.

"Well, I see the gang's all here. So, what happens now?"

The perpetually-grinning old man held out his arms, like a preacher about to deliver a sermon. "Now, we begin the ceremony."

Jonathan leaned close to Caesar. "I was afraid of this."

Hunter let go of Lisa, and took a step toward the altar. "Wait, before we start, do you mind if I ask a few questions?"

Aiden started to make a move with his Glock, but the old man held up his hand. "No, let him speak. There is no hurry and there is nothing he can do to stop the inevitable. Why should we not answer his questions? After all, he is a reporter, is he not? He can take the story to the world when we are finished. That is, if he is still alive."

Hunter stared at the old man, momentarily stunned that his delay tactics had actually worked, and a little uneasy about the answer itself. He quickly thought of something to ask. "Exactly who are you?"

The man furrowed his brow, as if disappointed in the question. "It makes no difference who I am. Those whom I serve are all that matters. But you may call me Oya. I am a Bokor, a priest of the Vodun house who serves the Loa with both hands. I have studied in your American universities, as well as in London. Once, I was even a professor of theology. But that was long ago."

"Those whom you serve?"

"The Great Old Ones. Some call them demons, cast down from heaven long ago. They once ruled the earth, even the universe, but they did blasphemous things, rebelling against the elder gods, and were cast down to the earth and sea. Some were banished to distant planets, along with their master, Cthuhlu."

Hunter shook his head in disbelief. "Listen, old man, I think you've been reading a little too much H. P. Lovecraft. Besides, you said you were a Voodoo priest."

Oya laughed. "It is true. But I have studied many religions, and virtually all contain one central theme—the struggle between good and evil, between the soul and the mind, the spirit and the flesh. And who is to say which shall win and which shall lose? Perhaps neither, or perhaps both."

Hunter thought Oya actually believed his own doubletalk, as crazy as it sounded. He was more than happy to let the old man continue, which gave Hunter more time to think of a plan.

The old priest gestured around the chamber. "In this very room, I have seen terrifying and amazing things that would make your hair stand on end. Yet, that is nothing compared to the things we shall witness on this day. We shall bring forth powers that will shake the very foundations of the world."

Hunter found the old man's proclamations a bit disturbing, so he decided to bring the subject down to a more mundane level. "I've seen the power that exists. The mere fact that a man who was once nothing more than a barnacle-encrusted bag of bones is now alive and well is enough to convince me that it's real. But I don't think you worked alone. I believe you had a little help in raising Blackbeard from the dead."

The old man nodded his head, his black dreads swaying with the movement. "You're quite right, my young friend. I enlisted the help of Mr. Aiden here, possessor of the skull of Blackbeard, as well as another person of your acquaintance."

Hunter turned and glared at Jonathan. "I knew it. You sleazy bastard. It was you all along, wasn't it?"

Jonathan stared back at Hunter in wide-eyed dismay, pointing a finger at himself. "Me? You think I had something to do with this?"

Caesar shook his head, putting a hand on Jonathan's shoulder. "I assure you, Mr. Singleton, my grandson had no part in raising Blackbeard from the dead. He does not possess enough knowledge of the black arts to do such a thing."

Hunter narrowed his eyes at Caesar.

Caesar slowly shook his head. "I know you think I may have had a hand in this, but believe me when I say I want no part in this. I only wish to stop it. I converted to Christianity long ago, and as you can see," Caesar swept a hand from chest to thigh, indicating his aging body, "the spell of eternal youth was broken."

Hunter was exasperated. He thought he had this thing all figured out. "Well, if not you, then who?"

As if on cue, someone hiding in the shadows of the passageway cleared his throat, and into the light of the chamber, flashlight in one hand and pistol in the other, stepped Jason Summerfield.

Jonathan, Lisa, and Hunter stared in shock at Summerfield. Even Caesar seemed astonished by this latest turn of events. Aiden simply kept his Glock trained on the group.

Blackbeard and Oya watched the proceedings with mild amusement, entertained by the drama unfolding before them.

Hunter found it difficult to speak. His face flushed with the anger of betrayal, but finally he managed to move his lips. "Tell me you just arrived in the nick of time to save us all, and that what I'm thinking is totally wrong."

Summerfield chuckled and shook his head. "You know, you steal my girl away from me, the only one I ever really loved, and you expect me to just forget it?" he said, his voice dripping with condescension.

"You mean this whole thing is about a woman?" Hunter glanced at Lisa. "No offense."

"None taken," she said, keeping her eyes on Summerfield.

"Besides," Hunter said to Summerfield, "you gave her up when you went your separate ways after school."

"I intended on getting her back, but that never happened, thanks to you." Summerfield shook his head, a sneer of contempt playing on his lips. "You don't really know as much about me as you think, Hunter, nor do you, Lisa. I spent many years here in the Caribbean, studying their culture, their language and their religion. I traveled the world and dabbled in other religions, discovering the darkest, most profound secrets of each, taking notes on them and eventually applying them in the real world. The things I accomplished were amazing. I created my own hybrid religion, combining the most powerful aspects of each to do what most would consider unthinkable."

Hunter's eyes bored into Summerfield. "Like raising the dead?"

Jason sneered. "Of course." He gestured at Jonathan. "Thanks to this man, I received an e-mail from a colleague in Raleigh who knew that I might be able to decipher the writing on a certain animal skin that Johnny here found on Blackbeard's old ship, the *Adventure*. It was written in an ancient code, a mixture of Latin and other languages used by old shamans to fool the authorities, and it just so happens I could read it."

Caesar looked at Jonathan, surprised by the revelation.

Jonathan's eyes flashed with rage. He moved towards Summerfield, but eyed the pistol and stopped short. "You sorry fuck, you killed my best friend. And for that, I'm going to kill you."

Jason Summerfield ignored the remark, as if it was only the barking of a chained dog, then continued his self-indulgent speech. "I knew when I saw that animal skin scroll that it was the break I had been waiting for. Teach had planted that scroll on the ship knowing that if anything ever happened to him, he would eventually be able to lure someone to the ship and they would find the bottle. Someone did. I have been studying with Oya for some time, and when we discussed our knowledge of Blackbeard's occult dealings, we realized that we could raise the demon and control it, at least temporarily.

"I went to Ocracoke Island and cast the spell from a deserted beach. I knew Teach would go after the skull first chance he got. Then it was just a matter of following him. Only the Death Defier knew where the secret book of spells was hidden. But even raising the dead is child's play compared to the things I have uncovered. There are beings that wait on the other side of the membrane, a wall which separates our universes, ready to reclaim their rightful place as the rulers of this world. And you," he gestured at Caesar, "are going to help us with your knowledge of the book."

"So where do Lisa and I fit into all this?" Hunter asked.

"I knew that if I brought you along on this quest, Lisa would follow, and Jonathan was my insurance that it would happen."

Jonathan shot Summerfield the finger.

Summerfield smiled at the gesture, then continued eyeing Hunter. "I knew that if I told you the story of the Diablero, your curiosity would be aroused. And I wanted you here to witness the resurrection of the Old Ones, and to have someone you love taken from you, as she was taken from me. Of course, I realize that Lisa will belong to Blackbeard, or whichever of the gods ends up with her. But at least I will have the satisfaction of knowing you won't have her."

Hunter resisted the urge to lunge for his ex-friend and rip his heart from his chest. Instead, he tried to focus on Summerfield's words. "You're saying that the Death Defier is one of the Dark Old Ones?"

"Most people just call them demons, which they are, essentially. But yes, Blackbeard is possessed by what is known in some cultures as the Death Defier, a spirit that usually walks the earth in human form, but also has power to move animate or inanimate objects, transform into an animal, or even raise the dead. But you already know all that. Cthulhu lore also calls him the Haunter of Dreams or the Nightmare Walker. The name is unpronounceable. He is the key, the one who will beckon the others to return from their exile."

Hunter said, "I guess I have to ask this next question then, because this whole thing seems illogical to me. Why now? And how could you betray the entire human race? Your own family, your own friends?"

Summerfield was nonplussed by the question. "Do you really think things are going well on planet earth? Even in the chaos of their time, the Old Ones ruled a world unaffected by war and hatred, for nothing was as important as the fulfillment of one's every whim. The Death Defier has been content to walk the earth alone until now, but with the other demons by his side, he will literally rule the universe. And I intend to rule with him."

Hunter let out a humorless laugh. "Do you really think they're going to let you do that? A *human*? You'll be lucky if all they do is kill you, Jason. Have you ever asked yourself why no one, including the Death Defier, has tried to bring back these Great Old Ones? There's probably a good reason for that. Like maybe they knew something. Something Teach has obviously forgotten."

Summerfield raised the flashlight and tapped it against his temple. "It's all in what you know, my friend, it's all in what you know."

Blackbeard, having had his fill of the conversation, bellowed in the small chamber. "Enough! It's time to begin the ritual."

Everyone in the chamber watched anxiously as Blackbeard shifted his focus from Hunter and Summerfield's conversation to Caesar. Stepping directly in front of him, he handed Caesar the book. "The time has come, Caesar, for you to unlock the powers that will allow me to free the Old Ones from their bondage, so they may once again take their rightful place upon the earth."

Caesar took the book with a mixture of dread and reverence. He stared down at its grotesque cover, thinking that the eyes might suddenly flash open, bright red orbs insane with agony and infinite hatred. He thought back to the day when he had first been given the book by The Teacher, before he himself had presented it to Blackbeard as a gift. At that time, there had been no fear, only excitement at the prospect of what one could obtain from casting its spells. But in the years to follow, Caesar found that there was often a vast disparity between fantasy and reality.

Now, he stood at another threshold.

Caesar looked up at the pirate who had once been his friend, who had offered him a life free from the bondage of slavery. But in those eyes that burned with fire, he saw the demon, and knew that Edward Teach was no more. "I cannot do what you ask. I want no part of any spell that would bring other creatures such as you into the world."

Blackbeard had expected resistance, and was ready for it. Before anyone in the chamber had time to react, he suddenly disappeared and reappeared where Jonathan stood, grabbed him by the throat in one huge hand and hoisted him a foot off the ground. Jonathan's legs dangled uselessly as he struggled to breathe, wrapping his hands around an arm that might as well have been a tree trunk. Soon, his vision filled with multicolored stars.

Hunter started to make a move toward the pirate, but the sight of Aiden's Glock changed his mind.

Blackbeard turned to Caesar and began speaking slowly, as though he wanted to make his words very clear. "Those whom I destroy do not merely die, but are taken mind and spirit. Their soul becomes a part of me, experiencing every aspect of my existence. I suppose you could call it Hell, because it is utter torment for the victim. And they are powerless to stop me. Their release can only be gained through my death, and death is the one thing I intend to cheat. So, what shall it be, Caesar?"

Tears stung Caesar's eyes as he watched his grandson's life slowly drain out of him, and knew there was only one thing he could do.

He prayed that God would forgive his soul. "All right, damn you!"

Immediately, the demon dropped Jonathan, who fell to the dirt floor, coughing and gasping for breath. Hunter and Lisa ran to his side, helping him to his feet.

Lisa glared at Blackbeard, who watched impassively.

Hunter slapped Jonathan on the back, brushing off dust and dirt. "Hey, big guy, you okay?"

Jonathan, his hands on his knees and still unable to speak, nodded in reply.

Hunter stood with a hand on Jonathan's arm. "I guess I owe you an apology. Nowadays it's just getting harder to figure out who your friends are."

Jonathan straightened himself, testing his strength. He looked over at Hunter. "Don't worry about it. We all make mistakes." He rubbed his neck, still feeling a bit sore. "I guess I know how you felt, now."

Blackbeard turned to Caesar and Caesar knew there was no putting off the inevitable.

The two-hundred-and-seventy-foot medium endurance Coast Guard cutter *Mohawk*, on patrol out of Key West, Florida, slowly glided up alongside the drifting speedboat. The deck hands made quick work of securing lines overboard and fastened a ladder over the side, down to the boat's deck. Focused and on high alert, the gunner's mate kept the fifty-caliber machine-gun trained on the speedboat, ready for anything.

The ops boss, Lieutenant Corey Wilson, stared down over the starboard railing and wondered what in God's name could have caused the carnage on board the small boat. The men had obviously been pirates. AK-47s and Bowie knives lay scattered across the deck, as if they had been utterly useless against whatever had attacked them. Sharks circled the boat, though a little further away than before, wary of the new arrivals. Dried blood stained the side of the boat where it had dripped down in rivulets.

This happened recently, possibly just hours ago, Wilson thought. *If that were so, then the killer or killers would not have gone far,* though he knew the chances of finding them were practically zero.

Wilson looked over at Boatswain's Mate First Class Simmons. "Simmons, get a hold of Enderly and have him suit up in a HAZMAT suit. Get one for yourself and one for me, as well. We're going aboard to take a look around. Maybe we can at least figure out where these guys came from."

"Aye, sir."

Wilson knew Simmons was a little squeamish about dead bodies, but he was also extremely good at detective work. He was always Wilson's first choice when mysteries needed solving, and this looked to be one hell of a mystery.

Wilson removed his cap and ran a hand through his disappearing brown hair. He noticed the sun inching ever closer to the horizon. Only a few more hours and they would be working in the dark.

Simmons eventually returned with two HAZMAT suits and the medic Enderly in tow. The three men pulled on their splash suits and gloves, fitted their filtered face masks in place, and climbed over the side, one at a time.

Wilson turned to Simmons and Enderly. "Search their pockets and see if you can find any ID. Also, Enderly, try to figure out exactly what killed them. We'll take a look below deck, as well, and see if there are any survivors."

The two men nodded, then everyone went about their morbid tasks.

Enderly went directly to the port side of the boat, where a man lay with an arm hanging over the side. He turned the body over. The man's throat had a huge chunk missing. It still looked fresh, and the flesh around the hole was ragged and torn, as if something had taken a big bite out of him. The man also had a deep abdominal wound, which looked like it had been caused by some sort of four-clawed device, or a huge claw, like that of a lion. But who the hell would have a lion on board their boat? Maybe the drug smugglers were getting more creative with their methods of eliminating the competition. Somehow, though, Enderly didn't think that was the case. Something very bizarre happened here, and it gave him the willies.

Wilson was not having much luck finding IDs on any of the men. Pirates probably wouldn't have much use for it, anyway, he thought. The bodies, likely Haitians, were torn and mangled in a way he had seen only once before, when he had been stationed in Kodiak, Alaska. A buddy he had been camping with had been attacked and killed in his tent by a polar bear before the rest of the party managed to bring the huge beast down with rifles. Wilson had not only lost his lunch when he saw what remained of his friend, but went into shock and had required months of therapy to recover. This excursion was bringing back a lot of very bad memories.

As he came upon the next body, Wilson heard Simmons shouting from below deck. He and Enderly looked at each other, then scrambled to locate the sound. They found an open hatch inside the pilothouse, and saw Simmons crouched down under the deck plates in the engine room. He looked up at the Lieutenant.

"You're not gonna believe this, sir. We've got a live one."

As he spoke these words, one of the pirates crawled into view, and stared up from below, his eyes wide with fear and shock.

"*Kijan ou rele?*" Simmons asked the man in Haitian Creole, trying to find out his name. Simmons' grandparents had migrated from Haiti to the U.S., and Creole was still spoken at family gatherings. Simmons had heard the language most of his life and eventually, after conversing with his grandparents for many years, became fluent in it. In the Coast Guard, being multi-lingual often came in handy.

The pirate sat on the edge of an examination table in the *Mohawk's* sick bay, wearing camouflage pants, green T-shirt, and combat boots, all of which were stained with blood. His hair was braided in tight corn-rows and he wore a goatee. Eyes red-rimmed with exhaustion and fear. Simmons handed him a cup of coffee as Lieutenant Wilson looked on, arms folded across his chest. The Haitian took a drink of the strong brew and made a face at it. He refused to make eye contact with either of the men.

"*Kijan ou rele?*" Simmons asked again, hoping to prod the man into answering. So far, it didn't seem to be working.

Without looking up, the man answered. "*Kite mwen.*"

Wilson uncrossed his arms and gestured at the man. "What did he say?"

Simmons said, "He told me to leave him alone."

Wilson turned his gaze on the Haitian, but spoke to Simmons. "Tell him we know he's a pirate, and things will go easier if he'll just tell us what happened. There are a lot of dead bodies on board that boat that need explaining, and so far, he's the only one available. That could make him a murder suspect."

As if he understood the Lieutenant's meaning, the man

slowly looked up at Wilson, then glanced away. "*Yon batay*," he said. The man took a moment to think, then continued to speak. He raised his hands, trying to outline a large shape. "*Yon zonbi . . . yon . . . yon lougawou.*" The Haitian suddenly dropped his hands, as if this small gesture had sapped all of his energy, then took another sip of coffee.

Wilson glanced over at Simmons. "Well, what did he say?"

Simmons shook his head, took off his hat and scratched his scalp, looking like a man who had just been told a great riddle. "It doesn't make sense. His words are kind of stilted, but he just said, 'a battle,' and then, 'a ghost, a werewolf.' I think this guy might be a little loopy, sir. We might not be able to get much out of him."

Wilson thought about the wounds they had seen on the man's comrades and wondered if the Haitian was really crazy at all. Wilson called to the medic, who appeared from an adjacent compartment. "Enderly, look after our guest. I'll have MK2 Sykes take charge and post a detainee watch when you're all done with him."

"Aye, sir."

As Wilson and Simmons left the sick bay, Simmons' curiosity got the best of him. "Sir, what do you think he really saw on that boat? I mean, the words he spoke were words Haitian people only use to describe dark magic or evil beings, and to tell you the truth, he really didn't look like he was lying."

Wilson responded with a look of surprise. "Don't tell me you believed all that stuff he was spouting."

"Don't tell me *you* did, sir."

"I guess there are a lot of things in this world that don't always add up, but I'm not ready to believe in werewolves and vampires just yet."

Simmons said, "So, what do we do now?"

"Well, we talk to the captain, then get on the SATCOM and call District Seven in Miami for orders. We're going to need a fast patrol boat to take the Haitian boat in tow. D.C. will probably want to contact the Haitian consulate and let them know what we found."

"What *did* we find?"

Wilson stopped in the passageway "Just between you and me Simmons? Something mighty fucking strange."

Everyone watched in awed silence as Caesar used a large piece of white sidewalk chalk to draw the last point of a pentagram on the stony floor. A pure-white candle had been placed at each point. It reminded Hunter of a gothic horror movie he had seen on late-night television as a teenager, when life was less complicated and monsters only lived in his imagination. But he knew this was real, that the pentagram was no joke.

He glanced behind him and saw that Aiden remained vigilant, his Glock aimed at Hunter. No chance for escape, Hunter thought, even if he had a plan, which he didn't. He watched Caesar, feeling his strength slowly draining from him, his stomach knotted with anger and frustration.

A line from Dante's Inferno came into his mind unbidden. *Abandon hope, all ye who enter here.*

At last, Caesar stood and walked toward the altar where Oya had placed a caged white rabbit. Caesar reached in and grabbed the animal and carefully cradled it in one arm. He held out his other hand, and Oya placed a large dagger in it. Before Caesar could think about what he was doing, he lay the animal down on its side upon the stone altar and, with one deft swipe of the blade, hacked off the animal's head. Its legs twitched momentarily, as if trying to run away, then was still.

Clutching the rabbit by its front legs, Caesar moved to Blackbeard, grabbed an arm and led the demon pirate to the pentagram, standing him exactly in the center. He turned the rabbit upside down, letting the blood spill over the ground within the pentagram, then lay the carcass inside it. He gestured for the book, which Oya handed to him.

Caesar turned it over and removed a seal from its back.

The loose, leathery flesh sagged and Caesar pulled the book out.

Hunter could see the cover of the book from his vantage point, and marveled at it. It was deeply etched in crimson with words of an ancient language. Below it was something like the running skeleton Hunter had seen on Summerfield's computer—the Death Defier.

When Caesar opened the book, Hunter could see the pages were yellowed and ancient, and the writing and symbols written there looked indecipherable, like hundreds of jumbled pictograms. To Hunter it resembled a mix of Chinese and hieroglyphics. He was in awe that Caesar could actually make any sense out of it at all.

The sounds emanating from Caesar were words, but Hunter couldn't tell if they were benign or malignant. They were simply words, ambiguous in their nature.

"*Tanè sala te daka nolo soptomna . . .*"

Obviously, The Teacher whom Caesar had followed centuries before had taught him the language of the book, written in code and deciphered only by those of the true faith. The words were like music, mesmerizing and haunting in their eloquence, echoing off the chamber walls and filling their minds with strange visions of shapeless, ephemeral beings.

"*Dalæ mon laptre te daka nolo saptomna . . .*"

The group found themselves entranced by the spell, unable to break free of its power, swaying to an unheard rhythm. Hunter's body felt as if he was under the influence of a powerful hallucinogenic, and he thought he could hear drums, like those used in Voodoo rituals, pounding furiously, inviting the spirits to join them, to inhabit them. Earlier, Hunter had wondered why there were no other cult members, why Oya was alone in the cave. Now he realized that the old priest was likely shunned by practitioners of Vodun. His was dark magic, crossing forbidden lines, delving into areas considered taboo by most.

"*Sapta somo monlané te dankstra, sapta somo dela te*

djuna, mana, mana, mana . . ."

Hunter's mind filled with thoughts of brutality, of killing and maiming, of sexual wantonness and lust: things that sickened and disgusted him physically and spiritually. He thought of Aiden, impaled on a stalagmite, intestines gushing like dark red ribbons across the dirt floor. He imagined Oya, savagely beheaded, laying in a pool of his own blood, and Jason Summerfield . . . Jason, his so-called friend, tied to a stake and screaming from within a wall of flames. And Lisa . . .

"*Kjunta sula te daka nolo soptamna . . ."*

Hunter realized that the visions were the influence of the Great Old Ones, sending out psychic messages, letting the humans have a taste of things to come.

With all the power he could muster, Hunter cleared his mind and opened his eyes, glancing to his side where Blackbeard stood within the pentagram.

Caesar's voice began to grow more frantic, increasing in its volume, its intensity. "*Jelanda, kafora, salanta, te daka nolo soptamna, te daka nolo soptamna!"*

Blackbeard's body was surrounded by an aura, shimmering with colors Hunter had never imagined, spectrums he had never seen. Blackbeard stood perfectly still, unaffected by the psychological madness that had overtaken the rest of the group. Then, his eyes shot open and Hunter saw that they were not only bright red, but filled with light. Caesar had also noticed this and stopped his incantation. Almost immediately, the group felt their sanity return, and reality came back into focus.

That's when they heard the sounds from within the cave. Blackbeard, with eyes like twin balls of fire, walked toward it.

And as Hunter watched in horror, Lisa began walking with Blackbeard.

"Lisa, stop!"

Hunter reached out and grabbed Lisa by the arm. Immediately, Blackbeard turned and, without even touching him, sent Hunter flying across the chamber and into the stone wall. The impact knocked the air out of him, and with some effort, Hunter got to his hands and knees and fought to suck in a breath.

He looked up and caught a glimpse of Lisa—who seemed to be hypnotized—exiting the chamber into the cave. Aiden followed close behind, curious to see where the noises were coming from.

Hunter gathered his strength and stood, with help from Jonathan and Caesar, waiting a moment while the stars cleared from his head.

Jonathan gave him a pat on the back. "Things don't look too good right now, do they?"

Hunter slowly shook his head as he stared down at the dirt floor of the cave. "My friend, we are seriously fucked."

The pair turned toward the chamber door and followed the group out.

Hunter wished almost immediately that they hadn't, for what he saw in the outer cave made his skin crawl.

Row upon row of corpses. Some had mottled, gray skin, and appeared to be recently deceased. Others looked ancient, nothing but skeletons with pieces of ragged cloth hanging from their bones. All were either standing, or digging themselves out from under piles of rocks that had been built as makeshift graves. They waited like an unholy army of the dead preparing for battle. Hunter wondered when that battle would be.

The stench of decayed and rotting flesh sickened Hunter. He looked at Jonathan. "Blackbeard did this, didn't he?"

Jonathan said nothing, merely stood staring, awestruck by the power that could give life to the dead.

His answer came, instead, from Oya. "Yes, he has done this. These were once followers of the Great Old Ones, and they shall serve yet again, even in death, to reinstate the Old Ones' kingdom upon the earth. But a great many other things he will do before this night is finished."

"Great," Hunter mumbled. "I can hardly wait."

Blackbeard looked around the cave at his army, a sardonic grin on his face. He raised his hands high, the lanterns casting a long shadow across the cave floor like a tide rolling in across a black ocean. "Welcome, friends. You have waited long for this day, and now your patience is rewarded."

As they all looked on, about five feet from the ground a very small space between them and the grotesque army seemed to warp, as if the dim light was bending and reshaping.

Hunter pointed at the spot and said to Jonathan. "What the hell is that?"

Jonathan watched the spot, his mind reeling at the implications of what he was seeing. Unbelievably, the spot seemed to expand, and Jonathan's blood went cold. "If that's what I think it is, we are all in deep shit."

Hunter watched the spot, growing another few inches in the space of seconds, like a hole in a piece of fabric getting larger as the thread unraveled. "Well, what do you think it is?"

Jonathan let out a deep sigh. "I think it's a black hole."

Hunter eyed Jonathan incredulously. "A black hole? Wouldn't a black hole create a gravity field strong enough to kill all of us?"

Jonathan continued to study the anomaly as he said, "Normally, it would. But the demon possessing Blackbeard seems to have some kind of control over its power, luckily for us."

Rocks and dirt began to swirl on the floor of the cave, rotating around the hole, finding the opening, like dust sucked into a huge vacuum cleaner. In fact, Hunter realized that a black hole, like space, probably was a vacuum, and would not only draw them all into it, but would also crush them to nothing with its enormous gravity.

Hunter looked around at the others. Caesar, Oya, Summerfield, and Aiden all seemed mystified and mesmerized by the shapeless rip in the fabric of space and time, the unfathomable darkness within it holding untold secrets and harboring incomprehensible terrors. Blackbeard held his arms aloft, a conductor presiding over a terrifying symphony. The army of dead simply stood, waiting, watching. Even Lisa looked hypnotized, almost like a zombie, unable to move or even think for herself.

Teach suddenly spoke in his loud, booming voice, causing Hunter to jump. "Cthulhu, oh great priest and master of R'lyeh, Azathoth, Hastur, Ithaqua, come forth from your exile, back to the world you once called home, to reign and rule, to live as gods among men!"

Hunter listened with growing terror, knowing that inside that hole were demons far worse than Blackbeard, ready to rip the world apart at the seams.

And Hunter also realized something else. He had to act,

and there was no more time.

He suddenly had an idea. It was one he didn't particularly like, but he had little choice. While Blackbeard busied himself with his spell, and the others were distracted, Hunter stealthily made his way to Lisa's side. He gently grabbed her arm, and to his relief she responded, looking as if she had just awakened from a dream.

Lisa looked at Hunter, bewildered. "How did we get out here?" She looked at the scene playing out around her in the cave, then turned back to Hunter. "Never mind, I don't think I want to know."

Hunter could see shapes moving within the doorway. He remembered that black holes were often thought by physicists to be passageways to other dimensions, places populated by beings, possibly of higher intelligence than humans.

And, Hunter thought: unimaginably evil.

Then he began to realize that light could not escape a black hole's gravity, so if he could see the shape within it, that meant it wasn't a black hole, but some other anomaly, like a wormhole. That realization didn't make him feel any better.

The dust and rocks began to swirl around them. The air in the cave moved with it, creating a whirlwind, rushing past their ears.

He swallowed hard. "Lisa, I need to ask you to do something. I need you to talk to Blackbeard. He has feelings for you. In life, women were his greatest weakness. I believe somewhere inside his mind, Teach still exists, but he either can't, or won't, fight the thing that has possession of him."

Lisa stared at Hunter, wide-eyed with apprehension and fear.

Hunter gently put his hands on her shoulders. "Lisa, you're the only one who can do this. You've got to try. You have to convince Teach to fight the demon."

Lisa thought about the time in her cabin aboard the

boat, when she and Blackbeard had talked, and he had actually seemed human and vulnerable. And she remembered the dream. She slowly nodded her head in understanding, and Hunter released his grip. He looked deeply into her soft, brown eyes, perhaps, he thought, for the last time.

"I love you."

She smiled weakly. "I love you, too."

Then, she turned and, without looking back, walked toward Edward Teach.

Lisa knew as she approached the demon that this would probably be her last chance to get through to Blackbeard. The sight of the dead standing amidst the swirling maelstrom that surrounded her made her stomach tighten with fear, yet she forced herself to keep moving forward, step by dreadful step.

Blackbeard stared at her with a gaze so malevolent that Lisa felt she might wither and die. He had turned toward her without so much as moving a muscle, his body repositioning itself in space, as if time had skipped a beat as she walked. It frightened her to her very core to realize that not only could this demon destroy her physical body, but could likely drag her soul down into the depths. Could Blackbeard read her mind? She couldn't be sure, but she knew he could read eyes as well as body language.

His eyes were of a color she had never seen, red but not red, like a burning fire on an alien planet. His eyes nearly burned through her, and she wanted to run.

"I want to speak to Blackbeard, to Edward Teach," she managed to sputter.

The demon laughed, but the laugh was strange, like several voices in unison. The sound echoed off the cave walls, causing a dozen bats to dive from their hiding places among the stalactites and flee to another part of the cave, screeching as they went. The strange opening in space was shimmering in their midst, growing, shifting, causing a wind that felt almost like a tropical storm. Lisa wondered just how fast the whirlwind would go before it eventually sucked them all in.

"He belongs to me, and you belong to me, too!"

Lisa felt her feet leave the ground. She forced herself,

somehow, to remain calm and not be overcome by the fear she felt welling up inside her. She began to drift toward Blackbeard.

She felt her clothes being stripped from her body by unseen hands as she floated through the air. The garments fell to the floor of the cave, one item at a time, like a bizarre striptease. In less than a minute, except for her silver cross necklace, she was nude.

Hunter watched helplessly, knowing that to make a move would cause his death and possibly Lisa's, as well. He had to keep the faith and wait. The others in the group had all turned their attention toward Lisa and Blackbeard. Hunter noticed with disgust that Aiden was licking his lips, obviously enjoying the show. He made a mental note to kill Aiden with his bare hands.

Lisa floated a foot off the ground as the demon eyed her lustfully, looking her over like a side of beef in a slaughterhouse. She was mortified and felt a tremor course through her.

Stalagmites all around the cave floor suddenly began moving on their own, twitching and undulating back and forth, some going around in circles and others stretching up, as if reaching out to grab the nearest body.

"Teach!" she screamed. Then Lisa took another breath, raised her hand up, and closed it around her crucifix.

Calmly, she said his name. "Edward."

The look in Blackbeard's eyes wavered momentarily, appearing lost, confused.

Lisa took advantage of it. "Edward, you don't want to do this. These demons, the Old Ones, they aren't your friends. You are not one of them. They come from a world that knows nothing of love and honor, of duty and sacrifice. Their world is ruled by chaos and fear. Even as a pirate, as Blackbeard, you understood what it was to be human. These things, they aren't human, will never be human. Look at them!"

As Lisa floated before him, Blackbeard turned and

stared into the wormhole. From within the opening, which was now nearly a foot wide, a monstrous tentacle snaked through, feeling the air like a cockroach using an antenna to test its surroundings. As Lisa watched, she saw below the tentacle what looked like the burning red pupil of a huge, malicious eye.

And it looked directly at her.

Lisa closed her eyes tightly to block out the vision, then opened them and focused her attention on Blackbeard. "Edward, listen to me. You've been given another chance. After all these eons, you can make things right and redeem yourself. You can put an end to this, and save your own soul."

The stalagmites stopped their gyrations, as if someone had turned off a switch.

Suddenly, Oya was moving toward them. "Silence, woman! We have come too far to be stopped by some half-breed."

Oya looked toward Aiden and Summerfield. "Shut her up. Permanently."

Summerfield knew he didn't have the nerve to kill Lisa, but Aiden raised his gun and took aim. Though he would have liked a little fun beforehand, Aiden still felt somewhat gratified at getting revenge for the earlier injustice he had suffered because of Lisa.

He began to squeeze the trigger.

Suddenly, Aiden felt an excruciating pain in his stomach. He dropped the gun and glanced down, saw what appeared to be a bloody rope spilling from his body. His intestines.

His agonized wail turned Lisa's blood to ice.

Aiden looked to his left and saw one of the recent dead holding a long, curved knife—cold, pupil-less eyes staring into his. Aiden collapsed in the dirt like a broken marionette. His body convulsed for several minutes, then finally lay still.

"Leave her alone," Blackbeard said simply. Lisa felt relieved, and more vulnerable than she had ever felt in her life, hanging naked a foot off the ground and unable to move.

Blackbeard turned back to the hole that had now opened at least another half foot, and the wind inside the cave had to be blowing fifty miles per hour, Lisa thought. Rocks and dirt pelted her skin, each one stinging her like pellets from a BB-gun.

Another huge, strangely-colored tentacle reached out from the hole, slimy and alien, appearing to come from nowhere. A second eye became visible. Insane, ungodly howls began emanating from within the opening, howls sending terror through some in the group, but Summerfield and Oya seemed almost to revel in it.

To Lisa's dismay, Blackbeard raised his arms once again. "*Ithaqua, Mordiggian, Othuyeg, Rhan-Tegoth,* come forth, reveal yourselves, let yourselves be known."

Lisa thought she heard the least bit of uncertainty in Blackbeard's voice now, and she knew she had succeeded in sowing the seeds of doubt.

Now, she had to finish the job. "Edward."

Blackbeard slowly swiveled his head toward Lisa, the fire in his eyes now reduced to a glow.

"Edward, they're using you. Can't you see? They're using you to bring them into the world, and when they're done, they'll destroy you, just as they destroy every human. There will be no ruling beside them. The demon that possesses you will keep you enslaved for eternity. You'll never be free. Don't let them do it, Edward. Be the man that you once were, the man that I know you are. Defy them. Defy them as you once defied the world, and show them you won't go without a fight."

Blackbeard stared into her eyes, contemplating her words. Then, he softened, and she thought his face looked troubled, as if a great battle was being waged between his body and his soul.

Lisa's heart leapt as she slowly began descending. In seconds, her bare feet touched the cold floor of the cave, and she glanced at Hunter, who was now moving swiftly toward her. He grabbed hold of Lisa, steadying her, and glanced at Blackbeard.

The pirate looked at them, and Hunter saw in those eyes the recognition of fellow humans, and he knew Lisa had broken through.

Then, Blackbeard spoke his final word.

"Run."

As quickly as they could, Lisa and Hunter gathered Lisa's clothes from the cave floor. She pulled them on as they worked their way toward the others.

Jonathan eyed the pair. "So he's letting us go, just like that?"

Hunter looked at Oya and Summerfield, who seemed confused about what they should do. Hold them prisoner or let them go.

Hunter suddenly felt compassion for Summerfield, the man who had been his friend, or so he had thought. "Jason, don't get caught up in this. It's insane. It's like Lisa said. These things aren't human. Humans to them are nothing more than cattle, bred to be slaughtered." But Hunter could see he wasn't breaking through.

Summerfield raised his pistol, and, quick as lightning, Caesar snatched it out of his hand and turned the barrel on Summerfield and Oya. The pair stared at him, nonplussed by the turn of fortune.

Summerfield shook his head, a humorless smile forming on his lips. "Hunter, your God is weak. The world is already in chaos. War, famine, disease—the Great Old Ones knew nothing of these things. You're right, they aren't human, and that's their biggest virtue. They offer a world free from the shortcomings of mankind, a world where your every whim is satisfied. Instant gratification. Do as thou wilt."

"You forgot one part of that saying, Jason. Do as thou wilt as long as it harms none. Do you really think those things are just benevolent beings, waiting to grant your every wish? You better think again, my friend. They'll rip you apart the minute they break into our dimension."

The monstrous things inhabiting the wormhole seemed to hear them, and the eerie, otherworldly howling intensified. The wind inside the cave neared hurricane force, the stinging rocks and sand becoming almost unbearable.

Blackbeard turned and stared at the group, and Hunter could see his power to control the demon was nearly at an end. His eyes pleaded with them, telling them that this was their last chance, or they would have to face the consequences.

Hunter eyed Summerfield, and thought about forcing him out of the cave at gunpoint. But he knew that would be useless, and might cause them trouble if he were to escape.

Now, it was Lisa's turn to plead. "Jason, be reasonable. Come with us."

"Why, so I can watch you live happily-ever-after together? No thanks. I'll take my chances with them. Better to reign in Hell than serve in heaven."

Hunter shook his head, saddened by Summerfield's words, but helpless to do anything. "I hope you know what you're doing. Good luck, my friend."

Caesar said to Hunter, "Go. I'll make sure they don't follow, then I'll catch up with you."

Hunter nodded thanks at Caesar, then he, Jonathan, and Lisa started for the other side of the cave, and freedom. They cautiously waded through the army of corpses, who seemed not to notice them, but who only waited for the word that had yet to be given.

Teach watched as the wormhole grew to three feet, fading in and out like a television broadcast from a too-distant source, and shifting in shape like a living, breathing thing. On the other side were infinitely evil, hideous beings of monstrous proportions waiting for their chance to enter into the earthly realm. Some of the beings were slug-like creatures with multiple appendages, some had claws or tentacles, and still others were nothing more than gigantic worms with gaping, tooth-filled maws which devoured everything in their path. All were demons, like himself, banished from the three-dimensional universe before the age of Man by the Outer Gods, or by God Himself, for unspeakable acts of blasphemy.

But he had been given another chance. He had managed to maintain control of this body until it had been reanimated by Summerfield. He turned and looked at Summerfield and the priest, Oya. Summerfield had set him free, given him another chance at reigning supreme over this world, and he had intended to take it. But did he really owe Summerfield anything?

And the woman. The woman was right. He was nothing more than a habitat, a home for an entity that had taken over his body, mind, and soul and slowly wrested control of it away from him, until finally, he ended up at the bottom of the sea without a soul. Now, after three centuries, it still controlled him, but Lisa's words had turned on a switch, awakened his true spirit. Made him lucid and aware. Now, he was at a crossroads. Would he set his fellow demons free, to roam and ravage the earth as they once had before the age of the dinosaurs? Or would he allow his human side, his *heart,* to lead him?

Blackbeard recalled the days long ago when he was feared and respected, when he commanded great ships and crews, sailing the seas in freedom, taking what he wanted. Then, Caesar had met the master, the Death Defier. He rued the day when he had killed The Teacher and the demon had immediately turned on him and overtaken him. Because of the demon, Teach had never been allowed to find peace, to truly rest as he should have. And all the other souls the demon had taken still screamed for release, trapped inside, along with Teach himself.

But now, he had regained control, had become conscious again and managed to overcome the demon, releasing those captive souls. Still, he knew this was only temporary. The Death Defier's power was too strong, even for an extraordinary man like Teach.

He knew he had to act fast.

Snapping, crablike claws and tentacles began emerging from the ever-widening hole in space, and the strange howling and moaning became louder. The whirlwind of rocks and debris was now hurricane force, and it was all he could do to remain upright. The noise was deafening. Strange lights and electrical charges like small lightning bolts appeared around the outer edges of the hole.

Blackbeard turned toward the dead army and concentrated his will on them. Slowly, one by one, the pirates and others who had been followers of the Great Old Ones, began to move. Oya, Summerfield, and Caesar noticed this and watched as the ghastly mob moved toward them, then began to crowd around them.

Summerfield became unnerved that there were so many of them, and they seemed to be ushering the trio toward Blackbeard and the rip in space that hovered in their midst. They were getting much too close. The rustling sound the dead made as they moved, rotted limbs rubbing up against him, the nauseating stench, all was enough to drive him insane.

Oya was not bothered by the turn of events, and in fact,

seemed excited by it.

"Do not fight them, my son. It is an honor to be sacrificed to the great gods from beyond, to be ripped apart by them."

Then, Oya let out an insane laugh, a laugh that Summerfield felt sure could only come from a total lunatic. The old priest began to move spasmodically, as if he were possessed, dancing and jerking in a psychotic jig.

As they came within a yard of the black hole, a gigantic, deformed claw shot out from it and snapped Oya in two, as if he were an insect. Blood splattered the living corpses as the priest's body was cleaved. A pair of reddish-green tentacles greedily grabbed both halves of the body, pulling it inside the hole.

Blackbeard watched impassively, his eyes now not only void of light, but black as two empty sockets.

As the dead crowded around, the smell of their rotting flesh and bones nearly choking him, Summerfield regained his senses, and decided he had seen enough. He turned and tried to make his way through the crowd, but there were too many.

Snakelike tendrils and smooth, slime-covered tentacles grabbed and probed at the dead, dragging them inside the hole, devouring them in ravenous hunger. Summerfield heard the sounds of crunching bones and eerie howls of ecstatic joy as the demons were sated. He watched in rising disgust as another tentacle grabbed the eviscerated body of John Aiden, picking it up and inspecting it like a tempting morsel.

Summerfield fought, scratching and clawing at decayed flesh, desperately trying to get through, trying to get as far as possible from the writhing black pit of Hell.

Then, his gut lurched and his heart sank as he felt something close around his leg. The grip was so powerful that it crushed his femur. Summerfield screamed, a blood-curdling cry. He was hoisted into the air upside down, and he watched the ground disappear beneath him.

He could see Caesar far below taking shots at the arm, but to no effect. Then he saw one of the tendrils snake towards Caesar as the old man shot directly into the hole.

Summerfield's last thoughts before the thing ripped him apart was of his friend, Hunter, and Lisa's beautiful, brown eyes.

The hole in space and time was nearly four feet wide, and Blackbeard knew he could wait no longer. He turned and looked around at the dead as they milled mindlessly inside the cave, waiting for their next command. Many of them he had known in his previous life as a pirate, and they had served him well. Some had even been friends. He hoped that now they could truly rest in peace.

Blackbeard turned toward the shifting, shapeless hole as dirt and rocks pelted his face and hands, the wind howling in his ears. He walked to the doorway. The demon within his soul, the Death Defier, screamed in fury at its own imminent destruction, unable to comprehend its defeat.

Then, Teach stepped inside, disappearing into the void. Immediately, the doorway and the Great Old Ones, howling at the injustice of a rebirth denied, vanished, and all fell silent.

The dead, sensing there was no more need for them, solemnly crept back into their resting places of sandstone and rocks, and slept.

Carrying a flashlight and a lantern, Hunter, Lisa, and Jonathan slowly moved through the darkness of the cavern to where the old wooden ladder waited for them. Hunter prayed that the ladder still had enough strength left in it to bear the weight of all four of them before it collapsed.

Though it shook and wobbled precariously, it held.

Jonathan, the last one on the ladder, looked across the cave at the spot where Blackbeard, Summerfield, Oya, and Caesar had stood among the droves of reanimated corpses and the swirling maelstrom surrounding the wormhole.

That was when he saw Summerfield hoisted into the air and heard the gunshots.

Then he saw Caesar.

Jonathan immediately began descending the ladder.

Hunter looked down into the hole, surprised to see Jonathan vanishing into it.

"Jonathan, what are you doing?"

Jonathan looked up at Hunter's confused face. "One of those things has my grandfather. I've got to help him. Don't wait for me. Get Lisa out of here and go back to the boat. We don't need any more people killed!"

Jonathan shouted this last part as he finished descending the ladder, then hit the ground running with a flashlight lighting his way across the cave.

Lisa said, "Well, should we go after him?"

Hunter shook his head. "No. He's right. My job is to protect you, and that's what I'm going to do. Once we get to the boat, I'll come back."

Lisa thought about arguing, but instead, nodded reluctantly. She was too tired to fight anymore.

It was dark outside, and Hunter turned and led the way to the front door and out into the field.

The thick vines and bushes leading to the beach looked foreboding, and Hunter knew they would be even harder to get through in the dark. With the help of a full moon, he managed to find the trail they had hacked out earlier when they had first come, and he led the way through it. Thousands of frogs and crickets performed their nightly symphony all around them.

As they approached the beach, Hunter thought he could see lights. "Looks like we might have company. I just hope it's the good guys this time."

As they broke through onto the beach, several members of the Royal Bahamas Defense Force, dressed in blue uniforms and caps, swiveled their flashlights toward them. Everyone stared at each other in surprise, Hunter and Lisa shielding their eyes from the blinding light.

"Why is it the cavalry always shows up after the fact?" Lisa quipped.

Hunter grinned at her. "Hey, at least they showed up."

The soldiers, realizing the two were probably part of the group they had been looking for, ran to them and helped them walk across the beach to a waiting boat.

Hunter could see an anchored Coast Guard cutter farther out, its familiar orange-and-blue stripes reminding him of home and all that was good in life. He smiled and jerked a thumb back over his shoulder at the forest. "I need a few men to go back with me. There are still some people—"

A commotion suddenly erupted behind them, and the group turned to see two people emerge from the trees.

Jonathan and Caesar.

Hunter shook his head and grinned.

"I thought you two would never make it. I was about to come back for you. What happened?"

Jonathan was out of breath. "I found Grandfather walking back through the cave."

Caesar grinned. "I shot one of those things in the eye. It

never even touched me."

Hunter frowned. "And Jason?"

"Gone, along with Oya and Blackbeard," Caesar said. "And the door to Hell has been closed, hopefully forever."

On board the small boat waiting to ferry them to the cutter, Lisa was surprised to see a familiar face. Though he wore jeans and a T-shirt in lieu of a uniform, Lisa immediately recognized Sheriff Jimmy Sutton.

Lisa looked at the smiling Sutton with bewildered eyes, then decided to forgo the formalities and gave him a hug. The boat pulled away from the pier as Lisa stepped back to look at him. She glanced at the two yachts tied to the other side of the pier and thought of Summerfield. And Blackbeard. "This may sound like a stupid question, but how did you find us?" she asked.

Sutton shook his head. "To tell you the truth, it was a long shot, and I would have really looked like an idiot if you wouldn't have been here. Thanks for not making a fool out of me."

Lisa smiled. "Glad I could help. Seriously, though, how did you find us?"

"I got a call from your dad, who was very worried about you. Said he'd received a text message from you. He's on board the cutter."

"Dad came along, too?"

"Couldn't stop him, as a matter of fact. Apparently, your dad has a lot of friends, even in the Coast Guard. An old buddy of his is the father of one of the officers, Lieutenant Wilson."

"So, he figured out the text message, huh?"

"It wasn't too hard. There aren't a lot of places in the world called Cat Island. Your dad called the Coast Guard and they hooked us up with Lieutenant Wilson."

Lisa smiled as she envisioned her Chinese father smooth-talking his way onto the Coast Guard cutter. "Leave it to Dad."

"The crew also found a boat full of dead Haitian pirates earlier today. One was still alive and he told a pretty bizarre story. That guy with the black beard was the killer, wasn't he?"

Lisa simply nodded.

"So what happened? Is he dead?"

Lisa felt weak, exhausted from the ordeal. She looked to the east, just as the sun was beginning to peek over the horizon. "To tell you the truth, it's a long, complicated story, and you probably wouldn't believe half of it. You'll likely have to send somebody down in the cave to investigate, but my guess is you won't find anything. Just some old bones, some candles and maybe a book."

Sutton glanced around at the others, thinking he had never seen such a worn and haggard-looking bunch. Their faces and arms were scratched from the thicket, their clothes torn and tattered. They stood in silence, seemingly satisfied with letting Lisa do all the talking. Sutton shook his head. "Looks like you all have been through hell."

Hunter put one arm around Lisa, pulling her close, and let out a sigh. "Yeah, sheriff, you could say that. You could *definitely* say that."

Epilogue
One week later

Liang helped his daughter carry the last of her belongings from her Subaru to the quaint, two-story Cape Cod in the middle of town. Lisa had moved out of this house months ago, leaving it for Hunter. The sun was bright overhead in the mid-afternoon sky, and though the temperature was a little on the warm side, Lisa didn't mind. She was just glad to be back home.

Liang glanced at her. "So, have you heard about what they found in the cave?"

Lisa had been so caught up in getting back together with Hunter, she hadn't had much time to think about it. "No. What did they find?"

Liang smiled. "It was just like you said. Nothing but old bones."

Lisa nodded as she climbed the steps up to the front porch of the old house. "Doesn't surprise me. Is Mom coming by later?"

"I'll be picking her up in a little while."

Hunter came into view as they walked into the kitchen. He smiled at them. "Hey, don't put your back out carrying that stuff," he said to Liang.

The old man smirked at him "I don't see you doing much carrying, Mr. Smartass."

"I'm more of a manager than a worker, per se."

Lisa walked directly to Hunter and shoved the box of clothes she was carrying into his arms. A look of surprise crossed his face as Lisa smiled impishly.

"Looks like I have a little training to do to get you back

into shape."

"Hey, I'm ready when you are."

The two shared a kiss over the box as Liang rolled his eyes and placed his own box on the kitchen table.

"If my wife talked to me that way . . ." Liang began.

Lisa looked over at her father, crossing her arms. "You'd do *what*?"

He glanced at her, suddenly at a loss for words. "Uh, nothing, honey."

Lisa laughed. "That's what I thought."

She turned and left the room as the two men looked at each other and grinned.

"Would you like some coffee?" Hunter asked Liang.

Liang pulled out a chair and took a seat at the kitchen table. "No, I'm fine."

Lisa's father, a retired River City police detective, had come to America from Hong Kong in the '70s looking for opportunity and love, and had managed to find both. A black-belt master in Kung Fu, like both his daughter and Hunter, Liang decided that law enforcement would be his chosen profession, and after a few years of learning English and working for a friend in a local Chinese restaurant, he tried out for the police force. With his jet-black hair and eyes, the local citizenry were a little reluctant to accept a foreigner as a local cop, but Liang's amiable demeanor soon won them over. Eventually, he got his degree in law enforcement and went on to become a detective.

The biggest challenge for Liang came when he met Lisa's mother, Elizabeth Moore, the black daughter of a fellow police officer. Elizabeth's dating a Chinese man didn't set well with some in her family, but her parents were surprisingly accepting of Liang, welcoming him as part of the family when he asked for Elizabeth's hand in marriage. It made family reunions quite interesting on both sides.

"So, how did your editor like the story?" Liang asked with a smile and an amused gleam in his eye.

Hunter gave him a half smile. "About as well as I thought he would. Stanton threatened to send me on a permanent vacation if I tried to file the story, so I'll just sit on it for now. I guess I wouldn't believe it either."

On the island of Nassau, Bahamas, a government official strode down the hall of the pink, colonial-style building in Parliament Square. As he entered his office, he closed the door behind him and walked over to the large, oak desk by the window. Outside, he could see the statue of Queen Victoria standing in the square. A palm tree swayed in the breeze as a motorcyclist passed, revving his engine as he pulled up to the building.

Though the man was relatively young, he was also very well educated, and understood the ways of not only those in this small island nation, but also the ways of the world. He had come here from one of the outer islands to work in the government and climb his way up the ladder to a place of power, a place where he could sway the hearts and minds of the populace.

The official sighed and turned to a large bookcase. Reaching up to the top shelf, he removed a book, and behind that book, recessed into the wall itself, was another book. He gingerly slid it from its hiding place and placed it on the desk.

He was both awed and sickened by the cover, crafted from the once-living face of an unfortunate human. He removed the seal from the back and let the cover fall to the desk.

The man stared, transfixed by the Death Defier depicted by an etching on the front of the book, and by the indecipherable words below it.

But the man knew that given the time, and the patience, he would eventually decipher it, and its secrets would be his.

He pulled out the desk chair and sat, then carefully opened the book and began to read.

 THE END

About the Author

Toby Tate has been a writer since the age of 12, when he first began writing short stories and publishing his own movie monster magazine. He started at least two other novels, but *DIABLERO* is the first one to make it to the finish line.

An Air Force brat who never lived in one place more than five years, Toby joined the Navy soon after high school and ended up on the east coast. He has since worked as a cab driver, a pizza delivery man, a phone solicitor, a shipyard technician, a government contractor, a retail music salesman, a bookseller, a cell phone salesman, a recording studio engineer, a graphic designer, and a newspaper reporter. Toby is also a songwriter and musician. He currently lives near the Dismal Swamp in northeastern North Carolina.

You can find his musings on the Web at:

> www.tobytatestories.com

… and his music at: www.tomrosemusic.com.

Acknowledgments

It would have been impossible to write this book by myself, so I want to give credit where credit is due. First of all, I want to thank my wife, Laura, and daughter, Zoe, the lights of my life and my inspiration, and my friend, novelist Stephen March for editing, for believing in me, and for always urging me over that next hill.

Special thanks to Dismal Swamp State Park Superintendent Joy Greenwood and Park Ranger Signa Williams for enduring my phone calls and interviews about their jobs and about the Dismal Swamp, and to historian Wanda McLean for pointing me in the right direction. Thanks also to my professors John Luton, Kip Branch and Joe Lisowski at Elizabeth City State University, my alma mater, for guiding me down the literary path to excellence.

Thanks to my colleagues at *The Daily Advance*, especially ex-Coastie Chris Day for answering my bizarre Coast Guard questions. And thanks, also, to my wonderful neighbors, Don and LuAnne Pendergraft, for reading my first draft and answering my weird questions about Blackbeard the Pirate.

I have to thank my friend from the days of Planet Music, Michelle Brown, for reading my final draft and for her encouragement. I have to also say thanks to Literary Agent Irene Webb for urging a rewrite of my rewrite. You were right.

Last, but not least, a shout-out to the extremely cool people at Nightbird Publishing, especially Jeff Dennis, a fellow musician and writer who believed in my book enough to make my dream a reality. Thanks, Jeff. Rock on.